The Mile High Club

Kinky Friedman lives with two cats, three dogs, a pet armadillo, a much used Smith-Corona typewriter and countless Montecrito No 2 cigar butts on a ranch in the Texas Hill Country. To order the Kinkster's new live cd, Classic Snatches From Europe, with Little Jewford call: 001 713 521 7700 or contact *www.sphincter-records.com.*

D1340213

KINKY FRIEDMAN

The Mile High Club

faber and faber

First published in the USA in 2000 by Simon & Schuster
First published in Great Britain in 2000
by Faber and Faber Limited
3 Queen Square London WC1N 3AU

Printed in England by Mackays of Chatham plc, Chatham, Kent

© Kinky Friedman, 2000

A CIP record for this book is available from the British Library

ISBN 0-571-20379-5

2 4 6 8 10 9 7 5 3 1

For Joe Heller

The Mile High Club

"Never sit at a table when you can stand at the bar."

— Ernest Hemingway

Midnight in the Sky

Italian heroes, American whores
Take up the aisles and emergency doors
The captain comes in and he straightens his tie
It's a quarter ever after Midnight in the Sky

If ever you lose someone that you love
You'll never get over, you'll just get above
Where dreams never end and love never dies
On a wing and a prayer, it's Midnight in the Sky

– from an unpublished song
by Kinky Friedman

1

" I F there's one thing I hate," I said to the beautiful woman on the airplane, "it's meeting a beautiful woman on an airplane."

"How terrible for you," she said, briefly looking up from her FAA-mandated copy of John Grisham's latest novel. The sleeves of her blouse were thin green stems. Her hands, holding the book, were fragile, off-white flowers bathed in the memory of moonlight. I glanced out the window of the plane but there was no moon. There was nothing out there at all. Not even an extremely tall Burma Shave sign. She was reading the book again.

"It was over twenty years ago," I said, "but every time I meet a gorgeous broad on a plane it reminds me of Veronica."

"Is this where I'm supposed to ask 'Who's Veronica?'" she said rather irritably, without looking up from the book. I was working religiously on my Bloody Mary, the third since we'd left Dallas. When I got to New York I planned to hit the ground running.

"Veronica Casillas," I said, staring straight ahead at the

painful past through the stained glass window of a broken heart. "She was a stewardess for Braniff Airlines."

"A *what* for *what?*" she said.

"A stewardess for Braniff Airlines," I said, as she closed her book and then closed her eyes. The FAA-mandated baby in the row directly behind us began crying. I could see Veronica, lithe, lovely, impossibly young, walking through an airport in a dream.

"Should've married her," I said. "But I let cocaine and ambition and geography get in the way. Because I knew I was going to be a star I guess I never really took the time to make a wish on one. By the time my country music career started to head south I wasn't equipped to do much but drink Bloody Marys and meet beautiful women on airplanes. Are you Hispanic?"

"My father's side is Colombian."

"Can I have his phone number?"

"Try 1-800-HELL," she said. "He's dead."

I'd been down at the family ranch just outside of Kerrville, Texas, for a few weeks, ostensibly on sabbatical from a hectic spate of amateur crime-solving in New York. The most recent case in which I'd become embroiled, dubbed *Spanking Watson* by one rather disgruntled Steve Rambam, had been particularly unpleasant. It had started with my efforts to seek revenge against Winnie Katz, the lesbian dance instructor in the loft above my own at 199B Vandam Street. Toward this admittedly less than Christian goal, I'd managed to convince my friends, the Village Irregulars, that a dangerous investigation was taking place and that it was their duty to infiltrate Winnie's fiercely private Isle of Lesbos. The result of this unfortunate exercise was the unleashing of a campaign of real-life crime and terror aimed at the lesbians, the Irregulars, and, to a somewhat lesser degree, myself. The outcome was that a number of individuals from a number of sexual persuasions were currently no longer speaking to the Kinkster.

The young woman sitting next to me appeared also no longer to be speaking to the Kinkster. I didn't know her name, anything about the maternal side of her family, or why she was going to New York. Possibly we already had exhausted everything we had in common. Possibly she was tired of hearing about the lost love and loneliness of a country singer–turned–private investigator. Possibly she hated meeting fascinating middle-aged men on airplanes.

"You never know when you might need a private dick," I said, trying a different approach. "Here's my card."

"That *can't* really be your name," she protested, holding the card at a guarded distance as if it were a mucus sample.

"It's not my full name," I said in friendly, semiconspiratorial tones. "My full name is Richard Kinky "Big Dick" Friedman."

"I'll just call you Dick," she said dismissively, her eyes straying back to the John Grisham novel.

"What's your name?" I asked, after a short period of uneasy silence.

"Khadija."

"Beautiful, melodic name. Khadija. Does it mean anything?"

"It means 'Woman Who Understands Why You Have Trouble Meeting Chicks On Airplanes.'"

"You've got to admit it *is* amazing. Every time I meet a beautiful girl on an airplane it always turns into some kind of hideous, star-crossed relationship. Invariably, there's a tragic, unhappy ending."

"Don't get your hopes up," she said.

2

THERE'S something especially poignant about two passengers on a plane positioned pathetically close to each other yet failing to connect in any spiritually significant way, as so often happens as well within the flying hours of life itself. You could almost reach across the empty seat between you and take her hand in your own, but, of course, you don't. It'd be too soon, too late, too much, too little, too perfect. Yet, in the immortal words of former passenger John Lennon: "I want to hold your hand."

As every plane must eventually begin its descent, to every high-flying dream there must accrue as well a certain measure of what we rather euphemistically refer to as reality. The reality is that stewardesses are an extinct species; now they're all flight attendants. The reality is that Braniff Airlines has gone the way of the dodo bird, the Edsel, and the quaint early American notion of stopping to help a stranded traveler instead of cutting his throat. And Veronica Casillas? That bird has definitely flown. Whoever and wherever she is today, she will always live in a lost city in that archaeological dig I sometimes like to think of as my soul. The only thing she ever did wrong was to fall for a country singer on the road. It'd taken her memory twenty years, I thought, but it'd finally broken my heart.

"Will you keep an eye on this bag?" said Khadija. "I'll be right back."

"Okay," I said, holding out a few tobacco-flecked peppermints I'd found in my pocket. "You want one of these?"

"I never take candy from strangers," she said.

Then she stood gracefully, stretched sensuously like a cat, and headed down the aisle toward the back of the plane. Watching her walk away was an experience. She had that little French newsboy haircut that brings out the latent homosexual in every red-blooded American. She had a charming face, a charming ass, and she walked like a little bundle of tightly wound dynamite, which, I imagined, could explode if you could just find the right button. When she finally disappeared from sight, I stopped keeping a close eye on her and started keeping a close eye on her bag. There's a little fetishist in all of us, I suppose.

By the time I felt the wheels grope the tarmac I wasn't watching the girl or the bag. I was awakening from a mildly erotic, oddly satisfying dream in which I'd gone out to California and shot O.J. Simpson and raped Steven Spielberg. I was somewhat surprised to find that Khadija still had not returned to her seat. By the time the aircraft had pulled up to the gate she still hadn't come back from the dumper and I was starting to become just a tad concerned. I couldn't very well carry the damn bag around for the rest of my life like a hot pink imitation-leather albatross. Where the hell was the girl?

If you've ever tried to swim upstream against a large group of New Yorkers deplaning at La Guardia you know that it's only a little bit easier than duck hunting with a rake. So I sat my ground and watched the crowd flow by, slow, ruthless, relentless as sentient lava. Maybe I nodded out again, maybe I didn't. All I knew for sure was that the airplane had by now regurgitated almost the entire flotsam and jetsam of humanity and the damn woman had still not returned to her seat or picked up her bag. It seemed a shame, too. A little more time and she might've warmed up to me.

By this time the only passengers left on the plane were an old lady waiting for her wheelchair and an extended Pakistani family still futzing with their extended luggage. I got up, got my cowboy hat—which by now looked like a tortilla—out of the overhead bin, and walked to the back of the plane. There I encountered a rather harried female flight attendant who appeared to be impatiently waiting for the final passengers to disembark. Over her shoulder I carefully perused the little signs on the two lavatories and quickly observed that they were vacant. They didn't call me a private investigator for nothing.

"Can I help you, sir?" asked the flight attendant.

"I don't know," I said, looking into the little kitchen compartment. "Do you think you could run this large black tortilla through the microwave for me?"

I showed her my flattened skypiece but she wasn't having any. She positioned her rolling luggage carrier behind her and prepared to move through the aisle, which, unfortunately for her, I was still occupying. The possible threat of incurring little wheel marks all the way from your scrotum to your forehead can be an unnerving notion. Nonetheless, I stood my ground.

"Did you happen to notice a young woman with short dark hair going into or out of one of the bathrooms just as the plane was beginning its descent?"

"No, sir," she said dismissively. "No passenger's been back here since the plane began its descent. The exit is toward the front of the aircraft." For further emphasis, she pointed clearly in the direction she wished me to go.

"Anyone ever tell you you're pretty good at that?" I said.

Obviously, no one ever had because the woman continued to stand intransigently, pointing in humorless and constipated fashion toward the front of the plane. Obviously, she was no longer a stewardess; she was now a flight attendant. Obviously, I was no longer a passenger; I was now an asshole. Maybe I was mellowing, but it seemed like there was nothing more to be gleaned from what was already a fairly unpleasant situation, so I headed in the direction she was pointing before we both went down in flames.

I grabbed Khadija's little pink suitcase as I ankled it down the aisle, and briefly perused the luggage tag as I entered the ant farm that is La Guardia. Khadija's last name was Kejela. There was a midtown address on the tag as well as a phone number. I'd also given her my business card, so I felt fairly comfortable about leaving with the bag. I wouldn't want to take something that didn't belong to me. Even in New York it's important to be a good citizen.

As I waited to pick up my own busted valise at the baggage carousel, I looked around in vain for my comely, erstwhile fellow passenger. No sign of Khadija. Her sudden departure was peculiar, all right, but a lot of things in life are peculiar and that's why they call it life. What comes around goes around, I thought, watching the baggage carousel and trying to get my cowboy hat back in the shape God intended. It was not an easy proposition. And cowboy hat wearers, despite their generally cavalier attitude toward most matters sartorial, are keenly image-conscious about their particular skypieces. You don't want to board a plane in Dallas looking like Tom Mix and deplane in New York looking like Hayley Mills.

At last I found myself walking the chilly sidewalk toward the hack stand, smoking a big cigar, carrying my luggage and Khadija's little pink suitcase, and wearing a black cowboy hat that appeared to have been hit by a meteorite. After a short wait in line, I cut the burning end off the cigar, put what was left in my coat pocket, got in the hack, set my ears back, and headed for Manhattan.

"That's a nice cowboy hat you got," said the driver.

"It speaks highly of you," I said.

"That's also a cute little pink suitcase."

"Thank you for noticing," I said.

Further conversation became untenable as we hurtled at about 190 miles per hour toward the destination that invariably made any thinking human being wonder once again about the wisdom of our deal with the Indians.

3

MOST people come to New York for the same reason Humphrey Bogart went to Casablanca—they start out looking for a good corned beef sandwich and then they get sidetracked trying to find happiness. They wind up happy just to find a parking place. Of course, if you don't drive a car the situation can get even more problematic. All that being as it may, by the time most of us realize we're never going to grow up, we also begin to realize that happiness is a highly transitory state. It's kind of like hearing from someone you love who only seems to call you from airports.

The hack hurried from Hudson to a darkened Vandam Street, threaded the needle between two double-parked garbage trucks, and spit me out in front of 199B. As was my custom, I overtipped the driver, hoping he would like me. He said, "Thanks, chief," and drove off.

The luggage and I rode upward in the little freight elevator with the bare light bulb and we all got off at four. I unlocked the door, brought the bags inside the loft, hit the lights, and took a quick glance around the place. It looked like Kafka and Sylvia Plath had decided to set up housekeeping. The only signs of humanity anywhere midst the gloom were the large porcelain head of Sherlock Holmes on the desk and the little black wooden puppet head on the mantel above the fireplace. The puppet head, a born optimist, smiled because he'd been down so many times yet always got back up again. You had to admit he was a good egg. He wasn't, however, much bigger than an egg. In contrast, Sherlock never smiled. He'd given up any hope of finding a parking place a long time ago.

I lifted up his deerstalker cap and took a cigar out of his cranium. I lopped the butt off the cigar and lit it with a kitchen match, meticulously keeping the tip of the cigar above the level of the flame. I blew a purple plume of smoke heavenward in the direction of the now silent lesbian dance class. When it was quiet up there you knew something was going on. Nevertheless, I found it personally necessary to call Winnie, even though it was slightly past Cinderella time. I had to pick up the cat.

Even though Winnie sounded strangely out of breath, and acknowledged that she had company, she gamely acquiesced to my stopping by to retrieve my little feline friend, whom she'd been looking after while I'd been in Texas. Indeed, it appeared, my not always pleasant relationship with Winnie was riding a mild upturn. This was possible, in large part, to my aforementioned caper in which I'd successfully nabbed a mysterious intruder who'd been bringing terror to Winnie's life, one Michael Linguini. Though the caper had caused a rather tedious strain on my relationship with virtually all of the Village Irregulars, oddly, it had brought Winnie and me closer together. You can't please all the people all the time.

"Come in," said Winnie, moments later when I knocked on

her door. "Felicity, the cat, and I were just getting ready to have a little slumber party. Felicity, meet Kinky. Kinky's a private—uh—dick, I think they call it."

Felicity was sitting at the kitchen table wearing a completely open house-robe and absolutely nothing else. Like most heterosexual men, the sight of two lesbians together in the same room was enough to make me want to start masturbating like a monkey, not to mention that Felicity was one of the most beautiful women I'd ever seen in my life. Unfortunately, she had the bad habit of looking you right in the eye.

"What're you staring at?" Felicity said to me.

"Felicity!" said Winnie.

"I'm looking for the cat," I said, not wanting to referee a same-sex domestic tension convention.

"You have a sweet little pussy," said Felicity.

It was not at all clear to whom she was speaking, but I had to assume she was referring to the cat.

"People are always telling me that," I said. "Where is she?"

"She got run over by a garbage truck," said Felicity.

"Felicity!" said Winnie. "The cat's hiding in the bedroom, Kinky."

"You never let me have any fun," pouted Felicity, her robe falling even wider open.

"Well," I said, heading for the bedroom, "I'll just pick up the cat and be on my way. Thanks for watching her."

"Don't mention it," said Felicity.

If you've ever gone away on a trip and left a cat for a longer period of time than the cat finds appropriate, you know how hideously peeved and petulant said cat can behave upon your return. As it was, the cat ignored me implicitly when I entered the bedroom, and as I picked her up and carried her downstairs she favored me with a weary, resigned expression that I interpreted as the beginnings of a brief, feline campaign of Gandhi-like passive resistance. Nevertheless, I persevered and soon we were both back in the loft, the cat sitting upright on the desk facing directly away from me, myself standing upright at the kitchen counter pouring a rather generous medicinal shot of Jameson Irish Whiskey into the old bull's horn.

"Now that you're back in a somewhat more wholesome environment," I said as I killed the shot, "tell me about your adventures while I was away."

The cat, of course, said nothing. There is an undeniable kinship between cats and lesbians that may have something to do with mutual, almost total independence from man. This proud, independent spirit never fails to irritate man and, after a time, causes him, quite irrationally of course, to become jealous, envious, angry, bitter, melancholy, restless, lethargic, and drunk.

But all in all, despite the mild strain of separation, the two of us were not unhappy that night as we went to sleep in the loft. We were both well aware that happiness is a highly transitory state. Like when someone you love calls you from an airport.

4

T H E next morning as I was traversing the shortest line from my bed to the espresso machine, I damn near broke my neck when I tripped over a little pink suitcase. At first I couldn't even remember what it was doing in the loft. At that hour of the morning I often had a slight problem remembering what *I* was doing in the loft. Eventually, I continued on my previously filed flight plan to the espresso machine.

"Remind me," I said to the cat, "I've got to get that suitcase back to that woman."

The cat, of course, said nothing. She did, however, evince a rather inordinate amount of interest in the suitcase. Possibly she thought it was a new piece of designer furniture for the loft. She began trying to scratch the suitcase. This behavior didn't really bother me. For one thing, it wasn't my suitcase. For another, I knew that when a cat scratches an object it usually means that the cat likes that object. When a cat scratches a person, however, it does not, of itself, necessarily indicate a fondness for that particular person.

19

"Don't get too attached," I said. "Once I get this espresso machine jump-started, I'm going to give the woman a call."

The former portion of this stated intention proved to be a far easier proposition than the latter. It wasn't long at all before the large, shiny, commercial-size dingus which took up nearly a third of the little kitchen began hissing and cooing and billing in a language that only large shiny commercial-size espresso machines understand. Only Old World Italians who are older than the instrument itself can come close to conversing with espresso machines and most of them are in prison for tax fraud.

While the machine moved with liquid grace through various Latin declensions, I resurrected an old Cuban cigar from my Texas-shaped, Texas-size ashtray and together we walked hand in hand to the window which overlooked Vandam. The cat, as was her narrow habit, followed me and leapt up on the windowsill. We watched the bleak countenance of the street below. We studied the garbage trucks, moving sluggishly like punch-drunk fighters. We perused the pigeons, flapping frenetically around the rusty fire escape. We watched a cop, a garbageman, a wino, a passing lesbian. You didn't see many families walking along on Vandam Street. You didn't see many children playing on Vandam Street. That was the way the cat and I liked it. The way we figured it, a cop, a garbageman, a wino, and a passing lesbian pretty well said it all.

As I lit my first cigar of the day I reflected fleetingly upon Stephanie DuPont. She hated cigars. She didn't think all that highly of me either. The last time I'd seen her was after the successful conclusion of the *Spanking Watson* situation and just before she'd departed on one of her numerous and rather lavish vacations. I'd told her that however our relationship eventually evolved, at least we both knew that we'd always be friends. Her exact response to my comment had been: "You're hangin' by spit, Friedman."

"What do you think she meant by that?" I rather rhetorically asked of the cat. The cat, of course, had not heard the commentary preceding the sentiments expressed prior to the audible question, so she said nothing. If she'd heard what I'd been thinking she probably still wouldn't have seen fit to comment. The cat hated Stephanie DuPont, despised her two small dogs, Pyramus and Thisbe, and particularly disliked her new Maltese puppy, Baby Savannah Samet. Stephanie, it should be noted, was quite vocal in her opinions and rarely had a kind word for the cat either. The mild irony that appeared to be lost upon both of them was that they each consistently interacted with the Kinkster in almost precisely the same manner. That's why I loved them, I guess.

The espresso machine now began humming a fairly florid, Italian version of Merle Haggard's great song, "Silver Wings." This reminded me not only that the espresso was ready but that as a responsible American it was my God-given duty to see that the baggage I had taken was returned to its proper owner. The owner, I reflected, did have my card. If she'd wanted the baggage so badly she could've picked up the blower and given me a call. But life, it seemed, was never quite that simple. Like smoking cigars or drinking espresso, if you wanted to be a responsible American, you had to work at it.

With a hot cup of espresso in one hand, and a cigar in the other, I marched over to the desk, placed said contents of hands upon the desk, and retrieved the little pink suitcase from the dusty floor. I plucked the blower on the left from its somnolent cradle and punched in the number on the baggage tag. The number I'd dialed had been disconnected. The new number was given to me by the automated voice of a woman who sounded about as warm and friendly as Felicity the lesbian.

I dialed the new number. It, too, had been disconnected.

"Life is never quite that simple," I said to the cat.

The cat, of course, said nothing.

5

T H R E E cigars, five espressos, and one trip to Chinatown later, I was sitting at my desk rather languidly clipping my fingernails. I did this once every six months whether I needed to or not. Great men, I'd come to believe, did not pay great attention to their nails or cuticles. Howard Hughes did not cut his fingernails or toenails at all during the last years of his life but he did manage to watch the movie *Ice Station Zebra* two hundred and fifty-six times. Leonard Cohen places great mystical value in fingernail clippings. Bob Dylan belongs more closely to the Howard Hughes, Charles Manson school. I myself feel that it mildly empowers you to let your fingernails grow and pretend you're a lumberjack or a blue-ball trucker or something, especially if you don't have a real job.

My friend Louie Kemp is an Orthodox Jew who lives in Los Angeles, which is about as strange as a Buddhist living in Las Vegas or a street poet living in Dallas, but it probably happens more than we think and those people need those places. I was moving along at a fairly pleasant, comfortable clip just thinking about the time some years ago when I'd been a housepest in Louie Kemp's mansion overlooking an oceanside cliff in Pacific Palisades. The mansion on the hill has probably gone over the side by now, but I know Louie's still alive because I talked to him two weeks ago. Louie is such a strongly devoted believer in the God of the Old Testament that if all of Los Angeles went over the side, which might not be a bad idea, he'd probably be one of the chosen few who'd be saved, along with, of course, O.J. Simpson and Steven Spielberg.

There's worse things you can clip than fingernails, I thought, as I diligently clipped away that lazy afternoon in New York. There's wings, for instance. I remembered fondly one lazy afternoon in L.A. as I was busily clipping my nails in Louie's big house. Louie had managed to disengage himself from prayer long enough to observe my behavior and become highly agitato.

"I'd appreciate it if you wouldn't clip your nails in the house, Kinkster," said Louie, ever the polite, well-mannered host.

"Why not?" I asked, ever the polite, well-intentioned housepest. "I'll keep track of every one of these little boogers and I'll throw 'em away myself. What's the big deal? I dump in the house. I fart in the house—"

"It's against Jewish religious law, Kinky."

"It's against Jewish religious law to clip your fingernails in California?"

"It's against Jewish law to clip your fingernails inside a house."

"Lot of rules for such a small company," I said. "Where the hell does it say that?"

"In the Talmud," said Louie.

"You've got to be shittin' me. *That's* in the *Talmud?*"

"Do you want me to show you the passage?"

"That won't be necessary. What I want to know is why those ancient rabbis or whoever the hell wrote the Talmud would care if a guy trims his fingernails in a house in California? I mean didn't they have bigger fish to fry like floods and locusts and Philistines and everybody running around coveting their neighbor's ass? What's the reason for this rule?"

"You've got to remember that a lot of things in the Talmud were written a long time ago. They may or may not apply to today's world, but it's not our place to determine which should apply and which shouldn't. As a good Jew you should follow the letter of the law."

"So what's the reason for the damn rule?"

Louie winced slightly. Five thousand years of California sunshine flooded majestically through the big windows of the big house. Louie continued patiently.

"The Talmud says that if a fingernail or toenail clipping is on the floor and a pregnant woman walks by and steps on it, she may have a miscarriage."

I stared at Louie like somebody'd just hit me on the head with a hammer. He stared at me with a quiet intensity in his eyes. He wasn't kidding. Like the gracious housepest that I was, I quickly recovered from my state of incredulity.

"That makes perfect sense," I said. "Why didn't you tell me that sooner?"

At this juncture, the two red telephones on my desk mercifully rang, thereby snapping the neck of my little spiritual reverie and shotgunning me back to the secular present. I picked up the blower on the left.

"Start talkin'," I said.

"Mr. Friedman? Mr. Kinky Friedman?"

"Who wants to know?"

"This is Angus Tailwind from American Airlines Corporate Security. I wonder if you could help us out, sir?"

"Which way'd you come in?"

"That's a good one, sir. It really is. But we're trying to locate a passenger who flew with you from Dallas to New York yesterday evening. Her name is Khadija Kejela. You were seated in 11A. She was seated in 11C. Did you notice her?"

"She'd be a hard one to miss."

"Do you know how we could get in touch with her, sir?"

"I'm afraid not. I'm thinking she might be getting in touch with me soon."

"Excellent! When she does, could you just give us a call or have Ms. Kejela call us? It's really quite important that we get in touch with her. Our number is 1-800-FLY-UP-MY-ASS."

"If I hear from her I'll see that she gets the message. By the way, would you mind telling me what this is in regard to?"

"Certainly. We have her bag."

After the guy had hung up, I thought things over a bit. I was under the impression that *I* had her bag. I'd waited at the baggage carousel until all the bags were gone. Khadija hadn't shown and there was no bag left for the airline to be holding unless they'd removed it before it got to the carousel. Probably it was a typical mix-up or mistake. The whole thing could be resolved quite easily, I suspected, if Khadija would simply pick up the blower and give me a call.

As if on cue, the two red telephones on either side of the desk began to ring simultaneously. This was not really surprising since they were both attached to the same line. I'd done this originally as a way to sort of enhance the importance of any incoming wounded I might receive. These days, about the only thing they enhanced was the irritation of the cat when she was sleeping on the desk between them, as she was now.

I picked up the blower on the left. It still wasn't Khadija.

"Mr. Friedman," said an important-sounding man in a hurry. "You were a passenger last night on American flight Number

207 from Dallas, Texas, to La Guardia. You were seated on the plane next to a Ms. Khadija Kejela. Have you been in contact with her, Mr. Friedman?"

It was old news, but I wasn't going to let him push me around like a little red apple.

"Hold the weddin'," I said. "You're pretty well versed on the subject of me. Who the hell are you?"

"Rusty Dossier," said the man. "State Department."

"Okay, State Department. Spit it."

"It's just a routine matter we're looking into, Mr. Friedman. Have you been contacted by Ms. Kejela?"

"Not yet."

"If and when you are, please contact us, sir." He gave me a number. "Just ask for Rusty Dossier. State Department. OCT. You got that?"

"Got it."

"And if she contacts you before we're able to locate her, will you give her a message for us?"

"No prob," I said. "What's the message?"

"Tell her we have her luggage."

6

T H E new fireplace in the loft, like everything else in New York, was moderately dysfunctional. On good days it burned like Joan of Arc. But when the wind picked up a bit the living room often took on a distinct resemblance to Flanders Field. The cat, particularly, did not enjoy the smoke and would invariably retire to the bedroom closet in a serious snit. I would stumble through the acrid loft cursing Vinnie and Gepetto, the two Italian workmen who'd built the fireplace for nothing. The price, of course, had been right.

It was a chill, thankfully still, evening in New York, and the fireplace was burning beautifully, warming the loft and all of its habitants. The cat slept peacefully on the nearby davenport. The puppet head on the mantelpiece positively beamed in the reflected glow of the fire. Across the room on the desk even Sherlock's cold, gray eyes seemed now and again to pick up a little spark of bright insight beyond the understanding of anyone save a fictional detective.

As for myself, I sat beside the fire in an overstuffed easy chair handed down to me by my favorite Irish poet, Mike McGovern. When you furnish your place with hand-me-downs from Mike McGovern, you know you're in trouble. Indeed, there was a faint frisson of trouble in my mind at the moment and it bore a vague relationship to hand-me-downs, I suppose. I was thinking of all the unclaimed luggage of our lives. How you always wish you could stay in touch but the right people never seem to. Maybe there are no right people.

Not for a minute did I believe that Khadija Kejela could've disappeared into thin air. Nor did I think it very likely that she'd left three pieces of unclaimed baggage with three separate entities, one of which, of course, happened to be me. I had never heard of an airline calling a passenger regarding the unclaimed luggage of another passenger. I'd also never known the State Department to get into the business of locating lost luggage. Did the airline or the State Department really have a piece of this woman's unclaimed baggage? Or is that simply what you tell somebody you think might be in possession of the bag you're looking for?

With a sense of increasing uneasiness, I poured a shot of Jameson Irish Whiskey—the drink that kept the Irish from taking over the world—into the old bull's horn. I threw a toast to the smiling puppet head and killed the shot. Then I got up out of McGovern's chair, walked over to Khadija's suitcase, picked it up, and placed it flat on the desk.

"What is this little article of leftover luggage trying to tell us?" I said to the cat, who now also occupied the desk, her interest apparently piqued by the rather singular activity of my moving the suitcase from the floor to the desk.

The cat said nothing but appeared to be giving the piece of baggage her entire attention. As did Sherlock. As did I.

"For a little pink suitcase it seems to have a fairly sturdy locking mechanism," I said. "You'll notice it's one of these numerical combination locks. We could spin the numbers for the rest of our lives and never get the damn thing open. And I don't want to force the lock yet. I still think there's a very high likelihood the broad's going to call. How do we know this?"

The cat said nothing. She did not share my deep religious faith that Khadija would call, nor did she particularly care. She did, however, find the word "broad" to be rather pejorative.

"Whenever a person leaves behind his or her possessions," I explained to the cat, "it usually indicates that the person is either forgetful, a slob, or Christ-like, and sometimes, on rare occasions, all three at once. But if the subject in question is a *woman*, and if she leaves behind merely a *singular* article of debris, and if the party with whom she has left the article is a *man*, there is a ninety-nine point seven percent chance statistically that the whole fucking business is Freudian. Pardon my Shakespeare, of course."

The cat did not take this highly persuasive, modern example of deductive reasoning well. For one thing, she questioned my data. For another, she did not care a flea for Christ, Freud, or Shakespeare, and she was clearly allowing her vaunted instinct for curiosity to override that far more precious commodity of logic. She wanted me to open the damn suitcase. For my part, I strongly suspected that Khadija would call soon and I did not want to have to defend my having forced the lock on her luggage. Though I had to admit that I was becoming mildly curious as well as to the contents of the little pink suitcase.

My vaunted instinct for curiosity was about to override that far more precious commodity of logic when the phones rang. I collared the blower on the left.

"Start talkin'," I said.

"Kinky?" said the breathy voice. "It's Khadija."

"Khadija," I said rather expansively, for the benefit of the cat. "I was expecting your call."

"Things've been a little hectic lately. Let's get together tomorrow night. I'll fill you in on what's happened. I can't talk now."

I suggested that Khadija drop by the loft around eight o'clock the following night and then we could go from there and maybe get a big hairy steak or something. She said it sounded good. She'd be here at eight. I gave her the address. I didn't want to ask any hard questions. I believed in letting a woman explain her own behavior first. Then I asked the hard questions. By that time, of course, there was usually very little left of the relationship but at least there might be some answers.

"Oh, by the way," said Khadija, as an afterthought. "Did you pick up my bag?"

I told her I had her bag. I did not tell her about the two phone calls regarding the bag. That could wait until tomorrow night, I figured. I'd have to wait, too. Though I had to admit there was something about Khadija's jet black eyes that appealed to the Gypsy in my soul.

"I'll guard your little pink suitcase with my life," I said just before I cradled the blower. Never in my freakiest agenda, however, did I even dream that it might actually come to that.

So I put the suitcase back on the floor and I poured another Jameson's and I walked over to the midnight window and poured the shot down my neck. Then almost without thinking, I took out my nail clippers and tidied up the earlier job on one particularly offending finger. Then slowly, methodically, almost without believing, I let the fingernail fall to the floor.

7

W O M E N , or so it seems to me, have a great deal in common with racehorses. Both breeds are expensive, excitable, fun to watch, and there isn't a man alive, regardless of experience, who can tell which ones will disappoint and which ones will come through for you. Khadija did not show up at the loft the following night. She didn't win, place, or show, or even deign to call me on the blower to say she wasn't coming. It wasn't that I had a lot riding upon our little proposed rendezvous that evening. Life would go on, I supposed. There would be other Khadijas and they would probably leave other little pink suitcases scattered softly along the shoulder of the lost highway that was my life. The entire episode had merely reinforced a lesson that I had thought I'd learned a long time ago. Never bet on a long shot.

Part of me still believed that Khadija would call that night. I had a few medicinal rounds of Jameson's, smoked a Cuban Montecristo No. 2 cigar, and paced back and forth across the living room for a few hours and pretty soon I almost didn't give a damn.

After all, it wasn't as though I was in love with the girl. She was just some babe who I'd met on an airplane. She still hadn't told me how she'd managed to disappear from that airplane, but by this time I wasn't even sure that I wanted to know. She was fairly accomplished at disappearing, it seemed. So were the contents, I noticed, of the bottle of Jameson Irish Whiskey.

Sometime after eleven o'clock the phones rang and I must confess that the first thing I thought of was Khadija. But it wasn't Khadija. It was, however, another racehorse. And this one, I'd known from the first time I'd seen her, was definitely a thoroughbred.

"Dickhead!" screamed Stephanie DuPont over the blower on the left. "I'm back!"

"How wonderful for you, darling," I said in rather clipped, bored, cosmopolitan tones. "Now where exactly was it that you went?"

"Don't try it, Friedman," she warned. "I'll put your ass on social probation and you won't be able to talk to me for six weeks."

"Anything but that."

"You know precisely where I go at this time every year. I go with my parents to the South of France—"

"Give your folks my regards—"

"That's the last act I'd perform on this planet."

"I can think of a few others I'd want you to perform."

"Putting your dick in the Cuisinart?"

"So what did you do in the South of France?"

"Twenty years into the conversation and you finally get around to talking about somebody besides yourself. We have a home there in St. Jean Cap Ferret. It's right next door to David Niven's house."

"How *is* David?"

"And Friedman, you're really in trouble now. You haven't even *asked* about Baby Savannah."

"How is our little love child?"

"Fine, Dickbrain. No thanks to you."

"Now you know Baby couldn't have stayed with me in the loft. The last time she was here the cat went right for her throat and if I hadn't acted quickly—"

"Your fucking cat would've gotten a ticket to Wimbledon as a tennis racket. I would've seen to it personally. Now lock that sick cat in the bedroom because Baby and I are coming down. I want you to see how much the little darling has grown."

"The cat's not going to like—"

But it was too late. Stephanie had already cradled the blower and no doubt she and Baby would be at the door in a matter of moments. The loft looked like hell. I was practically walking on my knuckles from the Jameson's. And the cat was staring at me with petulant challenge in her green, primeval eyes. The last place she wanted to be on earth was locked in the bedroom while a four-month-old Maltese pranced around the loft. It was not going to be an easy or a very pleasant operation.

I was just in the process of lighting a fresh cigar with what was left of my arm when I heard the knock on the door.

"Who's there?" I said.

"Very funny, hebe. Open up!"

Stephanie DuPont swirled into the loft like an Old Testament vision from a wet dream. Baby Savannah, whom she held in her arms, looked very much like a little white powder puff with sparkling black eyes and a tiny nose. Stephanie herself was now the possessor of a deep, apricot tan that made you want to lick her elbow. It nicely set off her shimmering white outfit and long, straight, blond, rich girl's hair.

"What whore left her Barbie suitcase here?" she said as she gazed around the place in mild revulsion.

"That's an interesting question, actually. I met this woman—"

"It looks like it was left over from the Louie Vuitton Death March."

"Yes, but doesn't it go nicely with the French country kitchen decor?"

"You met this woman, you were saying—"

"Yeah, I met her on the airplane and then she disappeared."

"Tell me what happened, Friedman. People don't disappear on airplanes."

"She was sitting right next to me. As the plane was beginning its descent she got up and walked to the back and when the plane landed she wasn't among the departing passengers. She seems just to have vanished into thin air."

"Maybe she got tired of hearing you talk about yourself and parachuted out over New Jersey."

"I'm telling you it was the wiggiest thing I've ever seen. I talked to the stewardess—"

"Flight attendant."

"I talked to the fucking flight attendant. There was no one left on the plane. I took her suitcase and waited at the baggage claim, but no Khadija."

"Khadija? What kind of name is that?"

"Her father was Colombian but I—"

"Friedman! She could be a drug dealer."

"I was hoping for an international terrorist. Especially after airline security and some nerd from the State Department called me yesterday—"

The conversation went no further along these lines because of a rather unfortunate interruption. Stephanie had placed Baby Savannah on the floor and, like any child of privilege, she'd taken to galloping, cavorting, and parading around the living room in close proximity to the bedroom door. At first, I thought a hook and ladder truck with siren blaring had double-parked next to the espresso machine. Then I realized that the rumbling, wailing, and scratching sounds were clearly emanating from high up on the door inside the bedroom. The entire loft seemed to reverberate with the unearthly din.

"We'll be on our way," said Stephanie, quickly scooping up Baby Savannah and heading for the hallway.

"Can we get together some night this week?" I said.

"It's going to be tough, Friedman. I've got a friend in town. Someone I met in France."

"Male or female?"

"Do I look like I've been watching *Ellen* reruns all vacation?"

The godawful noise from the bedroom continued unabated as Stephanie continued out the door, clutching Baby. In the hallway she turned for a moment, and standing there framed in the funky lighting of a New York stairwell, I thought that she had never looked more beautiful.

"One last word of advice, Dickhead."

"What?"

"Get rid of that suitcase."

8

I T was a mildly ironic situation but just as my relationships with the fairer sex appeared to be shriveling, several unexpected instances of male bonding came along to pierce the gloom of my heart. The first incident occurred as I was awakening the following morning, manifested by a loud and persistent knocking on the door of my loft. The cat and I, our relationship still somewhat strained by the events of the previous night, were not pleased by the intrusion.

"Kinkstah!" shouted an eminently recognizable voice. "Leap sideways, Kinkstah!"

I looked at the cat and the cat looked at me. From the frank, unbridled expression of disgust on the face of the cat it was obvious that the precise identity of the early morning caller was clearly known to her. His identity was also, of course, known to me.

"Kinkstah! C'mon, Kinkstah! Open up!" The familiar, rodent-like voice was now operating at even higher decibel levels if that were possible. This was not a nightmare. It was really happening.

"Goddamnit, Ratso," I said, as I stumbled on my sarong on the way to the door.

"All right, Kinkstah!" shouted Ratso, as I opened the door and he brushed past me into the loft. "How about a little espresso? Maybe a cannoli left over by those Italian guys who fixed your roof? How's the new fireplace working, by the way?"

"Ratso," I said, adjusting the sarong on my way to the espresso machine, "this is not a pastry shop in Little Italy. This is a private, residential loft. This company operates twenty-four hours a day, but we do not like surprises. How'd you get into the building anyway?"

"Passing lesbian."

"Sorry, Yorick," I said to the smiling puppet head on top of the mantelpiece. The key remained stoically in his mouth and the brightly colored parachute lay limp beside him. "There will be other mornings and other visitors for you."

"Probably in about seven years," said Ratso, looking around the dusty, desolate loft.

"You know, Ratso, the only reason I let you in at all is that you're an old friend and I'm sort of stuck with you. You know what I always say: You can pick your friends and you can pick your nose—"

"—But you can't wipe your friends off on your saddle," Ratso said, completing the sentiment for me. "At least I didn't find you *in* the saddle. I was pretty sure I wouldn't, of course. No offense, Kinkstah. But the only woman you seem remotely interested in these days is Stephanie and I saw her out dancing with some guy last night at an after-hours club."

"She told me she had a visiting friend in town."

"Visiting? You call that visiting? They were dancing pretty

close, Kinkstah. And in that club, I'd have to say they were slumming."

"I don't like to mention this, Ratso, but if the average person walked into any place you hang out, it'd be considered slumming. Stephanie can do what she wants. This is America."

"Then you ought to do what any good American would under the circumstances."

"Kill both of them?"

"Of course not. You don't kill 'em. You spy on 'em. It's been a while since the two of us have launched a real investigation together. You're the modern-day Sherlock Holmes with all your abilities of deductive reasoning. I'm the perfect Watson. I'm in touch with the street. I know all the places they'd probably be hanging out—"

"Forget it, Ratso. The whole thing's ridiculous."

"Speaking of hanging out and ridiculous, why is your sarong stuck out at a ninety-seven degree angle like that?"

"We call that a penis, Ratso. The sight of someone sporting a monstro-erection early in the morning while wearing a sarong is a rare and wonderful thing. You'll notice, however, as I'm speaking to you, that both the size and the angle are rapidly diminishing."

"Too bad we didn't think to try some time-lapse photography."

"Maybe I can set it up for your next visit. In the year 2010."

One of the nice things about Ratso was that nothing you could possibly say to or about him ever got under his skin. It merely rolled off his back like water off a duck. In fact, to my bleary eyes that morning, Ratso rather resembled a duck as he waddled curiously around the loft while I began the foreplay with the espresso machine.

For one thing, he was wearing a bright yellow slicker though it didn't appear to be raining outside. For another, the cap he was wearing had a bill on it about seventeen inches long. It was the kind of thing that might've been briefly fashionable amongst the wealthy young female tennis set of the twenties. On his feet he wore old-fashioned black high-top tennis shoes with bright yellow laces, possibly to go with the slicker. It was also possible that the tennis shoes, like many of Ratso's wheels, belonged to an individual unknown to him who was no longer with us.

It was some time later, after the espresso machine had hummed through a relentless number of fairly serviceable choruses of "Moon River," that Ratso and I finally sat down to a cup of espresso at the little kitchen table. Looking across the table at each other we realized the old friends we still were and undoubtedly would always be if life didn't get in the way. Little things like the money Ratso owed me and the rather spurious manner in which I'd solicited his involvement in the *Spanking Watson* caper, all seemed to flutter off like the pigeons outside the window. It was almost like old times.

"Nice new luggage, by the way," said Ratso, nodding at the little pink suitcase leaning up against the counter. "I kind of like that trendy off-lox color."

"It's not mine, Ratso. It belongs to a woman who disappeared on a plane."

Ratso quickly asked a long and tedious series of questions which I attempted to answer to the best of my strained abilities. He wanted to know What woman? What plane? What's in it? and Why don't you sell it? and I'd told him the whole story including the two rather peculiar phone calls I'd received from American Airlines and the State Department. About the only thing I didn't tell him was what was in it. I still didn't know.

"Jesus Christ," said Ratso, "there could be plutonium in there. Could be a shipment of cocaine—"

"Could be a shipment of the woman's undergarments," I said.

"That'd be even more exciting," said Ratso. "Let's open it, Sherlock!"

"Ah, Watson, your adventurous spirit is ever an inspiration! Be my guest."

"Fuck," said Ratso, as he studied the suitcase. "It looks like a very sturdy lock for such a small piece of luggage."

"Big rope," I said, as I refilled our espressos. "Small cow."

"It's got four dials on the lock. I'll try 1996."

"Very ingenious, Watson."

"I'll try the Jewish calendar year. What the hell is it? 5742?"

"Something like that," I said, "but she didn't look like a Jewish terrorist."

After futzing around with the dials for some time and finally resorting to an attempt to wedge a kitchen knife into the lock, Ratso gave up in frustration and disgust.

"I think we need to call a locksmith," he said.

"I've got a better idea."

"Rambam?"

"Who else? It's an interesting challenge, Watson, and an ironic little state of affairs. The world is hanging by a thread, mankind is dancing on a pinhead, my relationship with Stephanie is hanging by spit—to use her rather quaint description—and yet, my dear friend, this is a very strong little pink suitcase."

"Off-lox color," said Ratso thoughtfully. "You know, Sherlock, there's only one thing to do."

"What's that, Ratso? Trade it at a flea market for little Negro puppet heads and dead men's shoes?"

"Close," he said. "Sell it to the State Department."

"Except they claim they already have it."

"Use a little deductive reasoning, Sherlock. They *claim* they already have it, but they think you *might* have it, so they're

40

calling you, which means they obviously *don't* have it, so they must really *want* it!"

"Brilliant, Watson! I *will* get in touch with the State Department."

"Wonderful, Sherlock! But when?"

"Just as soon as I get this fucking suitcase opened."

9

R A T S O ' S large, luminous buttocks had barely walked out the door when I went to the blower and called Rambam. While Ratso was a good little Dr. Watson who brought a charming naïveté to any investigation, Rambam was the McCoy. He was a licensed private investigator who'd served time in federal never-never-land, was wanted in every state that began with an I, and was equally at home both inside and outside the law. Unfortunately, he wasn't at home. I left a moderately agitato message, cradled the blower, and lit either my second or my third cigar of the morning depending upon whether or not you wanted to count dead soldiers. I puffed impatiently on the cigar, walked over to the window, and thought fleetingly about Stephanie. That was the best way to think about her these days, I figured.

Ratso had started to describe her "friend" to me, but I'd cut him off in my haste not to hear about it. Now I didn't know if the guy was a British rock star or a Turkish diplomat. Maybe it was Baby Doc Duvalier. He lived in the South of France. All I remembered Ratso saying was that he didn't look like he was from around here. When "here" was New York, that was saying a lot.

"To love Stephanie," I said to the cat, "is to love Joan of Arc. To want to carry Anne Frank's books. To serenade Juliet on the fire escape. To sit on the beach in Hawaii with Princess Kaiulani and watch the green flash as the sun hits the sea. Love is always hopeless. That's why they call it love."

The cat, of course, did not respond to this tissue of horseshit sap city soliloquy. Cats rarely do. Cats are the people who elected Herbert Hoover. All cats have Sherlock Holmes's eyes. Cats are loners. Cats are realists. Cats are scientists. They do not fall prey to the toxic theme park of human emotions. And yet a cat in a mental hospital loved Van Gogh many lifetimes before the rest of the world and a dog loved Emily Dickinson—

But now the phones were ringing. I walked with quickened pace to the desk and collared the blower on the left.

"Leprosarium for Unwed Mothers," I said.

"Make it kind of quick," said Rambam. "I'm in Hoboken staking out the steam-cleaning of a Chinese junk."

"I've got a little situation here. I thought you might be able to help me out."

"After that last wild goose chase where you faked that death threat to Winnie Katz, why would I want to?"

"Temporary mental illness," I said. "Won't happen again. This one's for real, though. I even got a call from the State Department."

"*You* got a call from the State Department?" Rambam asked incredulously. "Maybe you'd better tell me about it."

I told Rambam about chatting up the woman on the plane, her subsequent disappearance in mid-flight, and her leaving behind her carry-on little pink suitcase.

"I'd give up my suitcase, too, not to see you again," said Rambam. "What happened next?"

43

"I couldn't find Khadija anywhere—that was her name—so after everyone had left the plane I took the suitcase."

"You're a fucking idiot. What happened next?"

"I called the number on her baggage tag and it'd been disconnected."

"Of course."

"Then American Airlines security called wanting information about her and when I asked why they said they had her bag."

"Which they don't because you have it."

"Right. Then the State Department called a while later dreideling me around with the same business. They had the bag, too."

"Of course. Did the State Department guy say what office he was with?"

"I think he mentioned some initials. OCT or something."

"Jesus fucking Christ! He's from the OCT?"

"That's what he said. What's the big deal?"

"Well, it's just that not too many people rate a call from the OCT. Have you had any visits from Yassir Arafat lately?"

"The only visitor I've had lately from the outside world has been Ratso. Come to think of it, he does look a little like Yassir Arafat. Maybe it was Yassir Arafat in Ratso drag—"

"Look, Kinky, this is no joke. The OCT is the Office to Combat Terrorism. These guys are not playing around. Taking that suitcase may have been the most foolhardy thing you've ever done in your life and it would have a lot of competition. If the OCT wants the suitcase you can bet the other side wants it, too. So we've got to find out what's inside it. Until we know what we're dealing with, your life could be in danger."

"Aren't you being a little melodramatic?"

"No. You're being an asshole. I'm trying to give you some good advice and from the looks of things you're going to need it. Now, if the State Department calls again—I can't get over there myself until this evening—so if they should call, just remember that it's a felony to lie to a federal agent. So just answer every question with another question."

"Like in the Talmud?"

"That's right, Rabbi Friedman. If you can't think of a question, just parrot their questions and drive them crazy. Don't lie on the record. In a situation like this, the State Department cowboys could be just as dangerous as whatever Third World Indians we're probably dealing with. So I wouldn't go anywhere and I wouldn't even answer the phone if I were you. I'll try to get there as soon as I can. I'm being deadly serious, Kinky."

Indeed, after I'd cradled the blower, I couldn't even remember a time when Rambam had sounded so serious. Maybe things were a bit dicier than I thought. But it all sounded a little too foreign intriguey to be true. A hell of a lot of excitement over one little pink suitcase. Whatever was happening, it was clearly over my head at the moment. And at the moment, the lesbian dance class, as if taking its cue, began a rhythmic pounding on the ceiling, which, of course, was over my head as well. I listened for a while and kind of liked the beat. I gave it a seven.

I had just taken a fresh cigar out of Sherlock Holmes's ceramic head and was beginning the prenuptial arrangements when I realized that the pounding was not only taking place upon the ceiling. There was also a pounding occurring upon the door. The two pounding patterns created a nice little counterpoint and I listened rather intently for a moment. Then I lit the cigar. Then I walked over to the door.

"Who's there?" I said.

"State Department," said the voice.

10

V E R Y quickly and very quietly, I grabbed the little pink
suitcase and spirited it into the rain room where I placed it beside the cat litter tray in the tub and then drew the shower curtain. When I wasn't taking my biannual shower I often left the
cat litter tray in the tub. It was a convenient, out-of-the-way
place for the suitcase as well. Nobody would think to look there
unless, of course, the cat had to take a Nixon and started raising
hell because of the unfamiliar aspects of the drawn curtain or
the neighboring suitcase. It was just a chance I would have to
take.

It isn't every day you get visitors from the State Department,
but when you do you always like for everything to be looking its
best. Unfortunately, there wasn't time for that. There wasn't time
for anything except to rush back and open the door. In a matter
of moments they had penetrated our perimeter. The cat clearly
was not pleased by the unexpected arrival of our visitors. I, of
course, was not pleased either, but I did my best to assume the

role of the perplexed, friendly, average, eager-to-please, church-going American that I personally despised.

"Well, well," I said enthusiastically, "come in! Come in! The State Department! This *is* an honor!"

There were two of them. They both wore gray suits. They both wore white shirts. They both wore red ties. They both wore sunglasses. They both had a practiced, easygoing, laconic manner that, though not directly, seemed to be vaguely, indefinably, incessantly nibbling away at the invisible human boundaries of fear and intimidation. They looked like a pair of something that hadn't been allowed on Noah's Ark.

"Good afternoon, Mr. Friedman," said the first one.

"You *are* Mr. Friedman?" said the second.

"I am Mr. Friedman," I said.

"James Ford," said the first one, displaying a small laminated ID card with his name, the word "Agent," and some other writing on it that I didn't bother to read. His red tie was good enough for me.

"Robert McKinley," said the second man, going through the same drill with the ID card.

"Why don't we all sit down?" said Ford, smiling like a dentist.

"Why *don't* we all sit down?" I responded Talmudically. It was kind of fun once you got the hang of it.

We pulled up the various mismatching furniture around the desk and we all sat down. I sat at my regular chair behind the desk. They both pulled up chairs to my left, but with the wall to my right, it felt very much like I was surrounded. The cat, I noticed, was watching the little interplay with close scrutiny from the sanctuary of her rocker on the far side of the living room. For once she did not appear to want to hang around the desk. These, she had already decided, were not her people.

"We'd just like to ask you a few questions," said Agent McKinley, his tones soothing.

47

"A few questions?" I said. Agent Ford fidgeted slightly in his chair. The Rambam Talmudic approach was already possibly beginning to get up his sleeve.

"About the woman who sat next to you on the flight from Dallas," he said.

"The flight from Dallas?"

"Our records indicate that three days ago you traveled from Dallas to New York on American Airlines flight Number 207," said Agent McKinley, like he was reading the back of a cereal box. "We are routinely looking into a small matter of another passenger on that flight who became separated from her luggage."

"Another passenger?"

"A woman seated in 11C," he said.

"A woman seated in 11C?"

"You were seated in 11A, Mr. Friedman," said Agent Ford rather pointedly.

"11A?" I said, as Ford's face reddened ever so slightly. "I'm sorry, I'm bad with numbers. Would you guys like a little something to cut the phlegm?"

I got up somewhat awkwardly and commandeered the Jameson's bottle, the bull's horn, and a few chipped coffee mugs. I set them up in a row on the desk and poured out three generous shots. I hoisted the bull's horn in a cheerful toast.

"To the State Department!" I said.

"Some other time," said Agent McKinley. "Can you describe the woman in 11C? Did she give you her name?"

"11C . . . 11C . . . Sorry, I'm lousy with names and faces." I killed the shot.

"What did you talk about on the flight?" asked Agent Ford with what might have been imperceptibly rising irritation. "It was a three-and-a-half-hour flight. You two must've had some conversation about something."

"Very little as I recall," I said, as I poured Agent Ford's shot down my neck. "I'm not kidding. I'm hopeless with women."

"Did you see a little bag?" slipped in Agent McKinley quickly.

"A little bag?" I said, as I killed McKinley's shot.

"A carry-on bag?" he persisted.

"Carry-on," I said, as if by deeply concentrating on that one word I could unravel the mysteries of the universe.

At last, there was a somewhat lengthy period of silence in the loft. I now felt I understood a little better what Rambam had been talking about. I could keep these guys here forever and they probably wouldn't mind. I could try the evasive Talmudic method until Elijah came back, but these two would not be rattled. They would persist. They would return. They would eventually prevail, as water over stone. As long as it takes would be as long as they'd take. And they would always be smooth, essentially emotionless, retentively ruthless until they got what they wanted. Rambam even had a phrase for this unique form of behavior. He called it the "federal bedside manner."

Soon both men stood up and I stood up a bit shakily with them. In spite of their great Easter Island stone faces I felt that I'd managed to at least mildly piss them off. Our discussion had been pretty much of a stalemate, I thought, but at least they didn't know any more about the suitcase than they had before they'd darkened my espresso machine. I followed them to the door.

"If we need any more information," said Agent Ford, as if the maddeningly futile ordeal had never taken place, "we'll get back in touch with you."

I stood in the open doorway as they walked into the hall.

"You'll get back in touch with me?" I said.

11

A B O U T fourteen minutes after the door slammed on the asses of the agents, I heard a shriek from the street that sounded like a large tropical macaw in heat. The cat and I went over to the window to have a look. We were mildly surprised to see Rambam's car with a green bubble light flashing parked on the sidewalk below the building. Rambam himself was parked four stories down directly below our kitchen window.

"Throw down that fuckin' puppet head," he shouted.

It was about time, I thought, that poor Yorick had an opportunity to get some air. Entirely too many people, possibly with the help of passing lesbians, were gaining entrance into the loft merely by knocking on the door. Why couldn't more people be like Rambam and practice the proper etiquette for entering the building?

"Throw down that fuckin' puppet head!" shouted Rambam again, this time quite a bit louder, if that were possible. A lady walking by with two children in hand shot Rambam a very nasty look, which, of course, did not faze him.

I opened the window a bit more and threw down the puppet head. The parachute billowed beautifully in a light breeze. The little black wooden head with the key to the building in its mouth drifted effortlessly like a buzzard in a Texas sky and came in for a perfect landing, dropping directly into Rambam's rather rapacious grasp. It was nice to see that the system still worked.

I pushed the window down and while I waited for Rambam I opened diplomatic relations with the espresso machine. Whether it was the three large rounds of Jameson's or the two large bullet-heads who'd just visited me, I couldn't say, but I suddenly felt ill at ease, highly agitato, and more distanced from my dreams than I'd felt in many years. The feeling was pervasive and foreboding and shunted my senses back to about the time Hank Williams had fallen out of my left nostril. The feeling hearkened back to when I'd been living at Ratso's apartment, doing large amounts of Peruvian marching powder, and writing my first Ratso-commissioned article for *High Times*, of which, at the time, he was editor. Those were the days when people died dancing. When they died in the fast lane with my latest love letter in their pocket. They, of course, were us, but we just didn't know it yet. Kacey and I never had a chance. Tom Baker conked at a quarter ever after midnight in the sky on an empty stage in a loft very similar to this one, except he wasn't in this one. Just the cat still looking at me for the chance to bust my chops with Baker's green Irish eyes. For Phil Ochs and Mike Bloomfield the last station of the cross had been Ratso's old skid-marked couch. That's where I'd written the piece for *High Times*. The article had been entitled "My Scrotum Flew Tourist: A Personal Odyssey." Now, many years later, the title of that article perfectly described how I felt. Like a shell-shocked soldier from the Silver War, I jumped at the pounding on my door.

"All right!" shouted Rambam. "I've got the fuckin' puppet head. Now open the fuckin' door!"

I scampered over, unlocked the door, and flung it open to reveal the puppet head's smiling face and Rambam's scowling one. Both of them walked into the loft, then Rambam flipped Yorick rather dangerously, I thought, in my direction. Fortunately, I caught him just as he was beginning his descent into La Guardia and positioned him comfortably back on top of the mantelpiece where he beamed at me beatifically. It was an oddly comforting experience.

"What the hell happened to you?" said Rambam. "You look like you've seen the ghost of Yom Kippur past."

"It's nothing," I said. "Probably just a touch of post-traumatic-stress syndrome."

"What was the stress? Did the cat vomit in your pipe again?"

"Worse. The State Department."

"The State Department vomited in your pipe?"

"They could've. They were here in the loft twenty-three minutes ago."

"They actually *came* here?"

"Not sexually."

"Kinky, this is even more serious than I thought. What'd you tell them?"

"Not a hell of a lot. The old Talmudic method worked rather effectively, I thought. They gave me their business cards in case I happen to remember anything."

"Don't."

I handed Rambam the two business cards. He studied them for a moment, then tossed them on the desk like a riverboat gambler.

"Ford and McKinley," he said. "They often take the names of former presidents. Typical fed humor."

"To paraphrase Mrs. Milton Berle, 'they weren't that funny at home.'"

"They're not even close to through with you. They won't stop until they get the suitcase. By the way, where *is* the suitcase?"

"Where is the suitcase?"

"Jesus, that conversation must have been tedious. Now, I'll ask you one more time. The feds have left the building. Or have they?"

I started to say something but Rambam put his hand up like a traffic cop and stopped me. In a low whisper he asked me if they'd walked around the loft at all. I whispered back that they'd parked themselves in the two chairs by the desk and remained there like two sedentary, humorless, constipated prigs.

Then Rambam got down on his hands and knees and began rather intimately feeling up the two chairs and the sides and bottom of the desk. He was either searching for a bugging device, impersonating Sherlock Holmes, or cookin' on another planet. As I watched the rather distasteful spectacle, it occurred to me that his bizarre behavior might've been the result of a little bit of all three. At last he stood up and dusted off his hands and his knees.

"Now where's the fucking suitcase?" he said.

"In the rain room. Right next to the cat litter."

"Remind me never to take a bubble bath in your tub."

53

12

"HERE'S your luggage, Mr. Rambam," I said, handing him the pink suitcase.

"Thank you, Rochester," said Rambam, placing the suitcase flat upon the kitchen counter.

He scrutinized the luggage for a long while like it was a laboratory frog. Without touching the lock mechanism, he studied the four numbered wheels. Then he looked at the little plastic-encased name tag hanging from the handle.

"I just remembered who Khadija was," he said.

"I told you. She was the woman who disappeared on the plane—"

"Not *that* Khadija. The original Khadija was Mohammed's first wife who died."

"Maybe that's why she stood me up the other night."

"Let's try setting all four wheels at zero. Most people don't bother putting in their own combination."

"Most people don't have two guys with red ties and sunglasses

54

scouring the landscape for their carry-on baggage. Maybe we should call the State Department and turn it in."

"Maybe we should call the mental hospital and turn you in. The State Department's already been here looking for the fucking bag and the fucking bag was here all the time they were here and you never told them a fucking thing about it. That's the way they'll see it. And you'll spend the next few years in the courts trying to clear your name and reputation, not that there's much left to clear. And it could get worse than that. You could become legally implicated in this and if it's serious enough you could go to prison. It happens all the time. Good little citizens like you go to prison and come out with an asshole the size of a walnut."

"All right, so I won't call the State Department."

"Four zeros doesn't work. Did you ever see my impersonation of a locksmith from Brooklyn?"

"Missed it," I said.

Rambam went over to the sink and I went over to the desk to fetch a fresh cigar out of Sherlock's head. I needed a fresh cigar. It'd been a trying day so far but, as Rambam had already rather graphically explained, things could be worse.

At about the same time, Rambam and I both started back toward the suitcase. In my hand was a cigar. In his, a kitchen knife.

"Hold the weddin'," I said. "There's still a fair chance Khadija may call again to get her bag. I don't want it damaged."

"Okay," said Rambam. "Then here's my impersonation of a locksmith from the Hamptons. But first I need a screwdriver."

"We're in luck. Vinnie and Gepetto left some tools here."

I was fishing around in the kitchen drawers when I realized that the espresso machine was muttering to itself rather violently so I drew two cups of the powerful brew and handed one to Rambam.

"This isn't a screwdriver," he said.

"This isn't Ace Hardware," I said. "Pace yourself."

I searched some more and finally found the screwdriver in the silverware drawer and brought it over to Rambam. He held it up to the light like a surgeon checking his scalpel. Then he placed it gently under the hasp of the lock. The cat, I noticed, had now jumped onto the counter to more closely observe the operation.

"You want to put just a little pressure against the hasp but not too much," he said, not taking his eyes off his work. "Now I turn the wheels one at a time very slowly while maintaining a steady pressure under the hasp, pulling gently away from the lock. Each wheel should stop at the appointed number. There's the first one."

"All *right*."

"There's the second one."

"Go, baby!"

"And—hold it, folks—there goes the third wheel."

"I can't watch! The tension's unbearable!"

"And in just a moment, ladies and gentlemen—this should be it—just a moment, ladies and gentlemen—we're experiencing a minor technical difficulty with this fourth wheel—"

"Sorry, you've exhausted my attention span. I've totally lost interest."

I was on my way back to the espresso machine for a second round when I heard the unmistakable sound of a suitcase unsnapping in a sparsely furnished loft in New York City. When I turned around I saw Rambam still holding the screwdriver and beaming like a local farmhand who'd just helped to deliver a child in a manger.

"That's fucking amazing," I said, truly impressed. "You really did it."

"Nothing to it," said Rambam. "It's a little trick I learned working twenty years in a Japanese suitcase factory."

The contents of the suitcase appeared to excite Rambam to a far greater degree than they excited me. I had to admit, however, that they were rather strange. Rambam took a sort of inventory.

"Okay," he said, "we have one vibrator."

"That's a stimulating discovery."

"It has three gears apparently."

"Does it have four-wheel drive?"

"We have some slinky black lace panties, stockings, and lingerie."

"Many terrorists shop at Victoria's Secret."

"We have men's socks, undershirts, underwear."

"Boxers or briefs?"

"Extremely brief briefs. Khadija may be a little kinky. Pardon the expression."

"If that's all that's in there, what's the big fuss about? That's pretty much standard contents for most carry-on luggage when the final destination is the Village."

"Yes, but they don't all include this," said Rambam, holding up a large plastic Baggie full of enough passports to make a customs agent put in for overtime.

Rambam opened the Baggie and we started sorting through the passports. There were about thirty of them, roughly evenly divided between those belonging to men and women. Some were U.S. passports, but many were for countries like Guatemala, the Dominican Republic, the Philippines, Ecuador, and the Congo. Most of the names and faces seemed to be of Middle Eastern origin, but not all of them.

"Considering that passport photos usually look like shit," I said, "this blonde is pretty hot."

"They're all pretty hot," said Rambam.

"So what do you think she's planning to do with all these? Sell them?"

"Hell, no," said Rambam. "I think you're looking at how the next bunch of World Trade Center bombers are planning to get away."

13

DUSK had fallen on the gray city by the time I was back at my desk with my feet propped up, smoking a cigar, listening to the lesbians, and watching Rambam furiously transcribing passport numbers into his little private investigator's notebook. If I'd been back in Texas it would've been about the time for the armadillos and other crepuscular creatures to begin coming out of nature's woodwork. Somewhere in the urban landscape of this city, I thought, still other crepuscular creatures were no doubt preparing to venture out into the wild. There was no way for a man to hold these creatures back, and if the man was truly a man he wouldn't really want to. One of them was Stephanie DuPont. The other was Khadija Kejela.

Maybe it was only a matter of pride, but it was moderately hurtful to the Kinkster that Stephanie, who lived one floor up in the same building, might be moving out of my reach and out of my life. I hardly knew Khadija, but she should've been a girl I met on a plane who flew close to my heart and grew to be someone ever dearer to me. But circumstances beyond both of our control had set her on a course of destruction to herself and others and sent her down a pernicious path I could not follow. Of course, I was mostly going on Ratso's report on Stephanie. And I was mainly operating on Rambam's suspicions of Khadija. I wished I could just sit down at some little Chinese coffee shop in Borneo during a long monsoon rain and talk with each of them, but one of them was a ball-buster and the other was an outlaw, and besides, what I'd told the State Department guy wasn't wrong: I was hopeless with women.

When it came down to it, probably everybody was. People didn't usually understand themselves, so how could they understand each other? We should all stick to things we were good at. Like armadillos, birds, dogs, cats, hats, cigars, stars, and feeling sorry for ourselves. Romeo and Juliet, Peter Pan and Wendy, Khadija and Kawlija—the wooden Indian; to understand a woman you almost had to be one. Maybe Winnie Katz was on to something. Unfortunately, it was too late for me to become a lesbian. Now I was just too old to die young and too smart to be happy.

This lonesome freight train of thought was thankfully derailed by Rambam, who'd finished with the passports and had to get back to Brooklyn to have sexual intercourse with a young Israeli aerobics instructor. It was dark out now and things were quiet upstairs.

"Okay," said Rambam, "the suitcase is locked and everything's back in it but the passports."

"The terrorists aren't going to like that."

"They're not going to find out until we figure out what to do next. In the meantime, stash the suitcase in the bedroom closet. Now we just need to decide what to do with the passports."

"Why don't you take them to Brooklyn with you?"

"Because they're thirty-five tickets to hell. Besides, you're the one who brought them into our lives. Where can you keep them safely in the loft?"

"I could try the old cat litter trick. It's worked before."

"Perfect. Keep them in the Baggie and bury them at the bottom of the cat litter tray. How often do you change the cat litter?"

"Once every seven years."

"Works for me," said Rambam, flipping the packet of passports in my direction. I almost caught the packet but it slipped through my grasp and fell heavily onto the floor.

"That's seven years of bad luck," said Rambam.

"Good," I said. "Then I'll know when to change the cat litter."

At the door, Rambam turned and looked at me sitting in my chair with the pile of passports burning a hole in the desk. It must have been a fairly pitiable sight because he made a rare inquiry as to my welfare.

"Are you going to be all right?"

"Sure," I said with a confidence I didn't feel. "Why do you think God sent these passports to me wrapped in a Baggie? Because He knew I was going to keep them in the cat litter tray."

"That could be true," said Rambam. "But there's still one thing that's worrying me."

"What's that?" I said, resurrecting a half-smoked cigar with a green Bic lighter that had been in the family for about forty-eight hours.

"If God knows," said Rambam, "so does Allah."

14

" T H E funny thing about that in-depth interview I did with Winnie Katz," said McGovern, "is that the *Times* of London really is going to run it."

"You're kidding," I said, as I nursed another Guinness. McGovern was slightly ahead of me, already working on either his third or fourth Vodka McGovern. We were at the Corner Bistro. It was half-past Cinderella time.

"I just told Winnie today," McGovern continued. "She's one very excited lesbian. The *Times* pays well, too, so it's all worked out okay in spite of the way you conned me into the whole operation."

"Don't rub it in," I said.

It felt good to be back on good terms with McGovern, just sitting and talking and sharing a few rounds at the old battle-scarred bar of the Bistro. The *Spanking Watson* caper had clearly created a major rift between me and my favorite Irish poet. I was happy to see that if all wasn't forgiven, at least most of the things that counted were.

"How're things going with your beautiful friend Stephanie?" McGovern asked innocently.

McGovern asked everything innocently, I thought, mainly because he was as innocent as anyone could be in this day and age and still be ambulatory. He was a genuinely good, well-meaning man, and that was probably why unpleasant things kept happening to him in New York. I wasn't sure what my excuse was.

"My beautiful friend Stephanie is being visited here in the city by a beautiful friend of hers whom she met in the South of France on her recent vacation."

"The South of France'll do it every time. It's a magical place."

"So's the men's room of the Monkey's Paw."

"I've scored in both," said McGovern.

"You're quite a cosmopolitan figure," I said, "but you might try zipping your fly."

"Thanks, pal," said McGovern, laughing heartily and attending to that particular procedure. "What would I do without you?"

"You'd probably walk around with your dick hanging out."

"Like they do in the South of France?"

"I'm starting not to like the South of France. I prefer the old-fashioned American values of the Village. Friendship, loyalty, love—"

"What village is that?" said McGovern, ordering us both another round.

"It's the village we had to destroy in order to save," I said.

Try as I might I couldn't get the image of Stephanie and her new friend out of my mind. Even the Guinness didn't seem to be helping. And if Guinness can't help you, as they say in Ireland, nothing can.

"Ratso saw the two of them out at some after-hours club the other night," I said. "His brilliant idea is for us to investigate. Spy on them. Find out who the guy is."

McGovern laughed again, a little too loudly, as usual. Then a dangerous, faraway look came into his eyes. I'd seen it before and it nearly always meant trouble.

"Wait a minute," he said. "I told you that the *Times* of London is running the piece I did on Winnie Katz?"

"You're starting to repeat yourself, McGovern."

"Well, they've also assigned me the story of Rambam and his exploits hunting Nazis in Canada. They're particularly interested in his untested, unconventional, high-tech methodologies. They see him as sort of a slightly twisted, real-life, American James Bond."

"Who do they see you as? Edward R. Murrow?"

"This could be a lark," McGovern prattled on obliviously. "The *Times* wants me to verify the effectiveness of the pen mike Rambam used to secretly record the Nazis."

"A pen mike? What the hell is that?"

"It's a little microphone inside a fucking ballpoint pen. Rambam also has his hands on something only the military's used up until now. It's called the NVD. Night vision device."

"How does Rambam obtain these things?"

"A good spy never reveals his sources. Neither does a good journalist."

"It's a wonder anybody ever finds out anything."

"There's one thing I bet we could find out," said McGovern.

"What's that? Whether or not Ratso wears underwear at midnight?"

"Hell no. We could find out for certain the identity of Stephanie's friend. We could also find out the precise nature and the relative seriousness of their relationship. It'd be a great way to test some of Rambam's new high-tech toys in an actual living theater of operations. We'd maintain a regular surveillance of Stephanie and the guy. See them when they think they're not being watched. Hear their most intimate conversations in restaurants and hotel rooms—"

"Hotel rooms?"

"Wherever. We'll follow them around for a few nights everywhere they go. Rambam will test his high-tech spy equipment. I'll get the story. You'll get the truth. Always provided, of course, that you want the truth."

I sat there at the bar like somebody had just hit me on the head with a croquet mallet. I did want the truth, didn't I? On the other hand, does anybody ever really want the truth? I mulled it over as McGovern ordered yet another round for both of us and wandered over to talk to a friend of his by the front window of the place. Was I just a man alone on a barstool drinking myself into oblivion? Had I come this far in life merely to hide from it? Did I not wish to know life as it was? Love as it was? Was I only a searcher, a seeker of truth in matters that didn't matter?

Besides, I thought, with thirty-five fraudulent terrorist passports lurking in the cat litter tray, the loft might not be the best place in the world in which to be hanging out. Now that I knew the potential danger of possessing the contents of Khadija's suitcase, I did not want to drag innocent children like McGovern and Ratso into what could turn into an extremely unpleasant situation. By going along with the surveillance of Stephanie and her friend, it would get my mind off the other, weightier matter, and might also provide the opportunity to at least be a moving target for the terrorists and/or the State Department.

Anyway you looked at it, spying on Stephanie was infinitely safer than waiting for Khadija. All someone like Stephanie could do to you was break your heart again and scientists have proven that never really happens to you more than once.

"I just called Rambam," said McGovern, suddenly looming

over my shoulder holding a tall Vodka McGovern. "We can start tomorrow night. Are you with us?"

I glanced briefly at the reflection of my face in the mirror behind the bar. I looked like the loneliest man I'd ever met.

"What do I have to lose?" I said.

15

I once knew a girl who kept missing planes. It's possible, looking back on things, that she didn't really want to leave. But that, of course, could just be wishful thinking on my part. For some reason, known only to God and Amelia Earhart, I've never missed a flight. God and Amelia have not told me why, but I sometimes arrive almost pathologically early at airports finding myself with several hours to kill while drinking coffee and walking around those miles of bathroom tiles watching people and dreams pass by like highway reflectors.

Maybe I like airports because they never sleep. The people in them are the children of the people you used to see in bus stations and train stations before they flew away to the stars. You see pieces of people's lives that'll never fit together again. You see lovers saying goodbye like in a storybook. Romeo, please report to the Alitalia information desk. Will the party meeting John Lennon please report to the nondenominational chapel? Will the driver of a 1953 sky blue Cadillac please return to your vehicle?

One of the more disappointing aspects of being at airports is that it's hard for you to receive calls unless you're a modern-day cell phone nerd. But you can call your answering machine or your voice mail and see if you called yourself from an airport. If you hear your own voice it may remind you that you're the most important person in the world who can call you from an airport because if you don't die trying to get out of your own way you'll never be who you always wanted to be when you grow up.

Airports are also sad. They know they can't effectively help us terminate the holding patterns of our lives. They're airports, not shrinks. What the hell do you expect? They know their coffee, bagels, popcorn, lighting, service, and decor are not the best. They also know that nobody gives a shit. They're only airports. Cathedrals to the absence of the earthbound soul. Sanctuaries surrounded by wings trying vainly to comfort the terminal among us, and who among us is not terminal?

Airports provide you with pictures of better places to be than Dallas. The best scenes are often seen in airports just like the best dreams are often dreamed in cheap motels. The girl who kept missing planes and I made love one magical Irving Berlin White Christmas California night at the Tropicana Motel in L.A. Like all star-crossed lovers, we lived in our dreams and dreamed of our lives like June bugs clinging to a summer screen or messages missed on answering machines.

She'd wanted me to protect her from animals that had attacked her in childhood nightmares. "What kind of animals?" I asked. "Bad animals," she said. I've just about lived twice as long as she ever did by now and I think I've finally figured out who the bad animals were. They weren't animals at all, really. They were just lawyers in Los Angeles.

In the morning both of us were still half stoned when she drove away in her little blue sports car to meet a bad animal. My friend Chuck E. Weiss and I watched her zim across the boule-vard at a land speed neither of us had ever dared. "We're wit-nessing the end of the fairy tale," he said.

That was the moment that I pretty much realized I was never going to be a prince. Chuck E. himself was never going to be a prince either. In third grade he'd once tried to pour a small bot-tle of cinnamon oil over the top of a neighboring toilet stall onto the buttocks of a little Negro classmate. It was not an act of racism. They'd been dipping toothpicks in the cinnamon oil, a grade school fad, and Chuck E. was something of a troublemaker even then, and if Gandhi had been in that stall at that time cleaning the toilet or something, Chuck E. would've poured the cinnamon oil on Gandhi's buttocks. It's a good thing it was the Negro instead of Gandhi because taking that ignoble action against the latter probably would've engendered about seven years of bad luck. Even Chuck E. didn't need that.

As it happened Chuck E. didn't even pour the cinnamon oil onto the Negro's buttocks. The kid looked up at the last minute and the oil went into his eyes whereupon the child rushed out of the dumper and into the classroom screaming to anyone who would listen: "Chuck E. *Weiss* poured cinnamon oil in my *eyes!* Chuck E. *Weiss* poured cinnamon oil in my *eyes!*" The way the kid pronounced it, "eyes" and "Weiss" rhymed perfectly.

The trouble with people who keep missing planes is that you have to keep saying goodbye to them until one day they're finally gone and you realize that all your life you've been busy dreaming or saying goodbye. It's just fortunate that airports are all con-nected to the same sky.

By the time I got up from my power nap on the davenport it was already early afternoon. If all went as planned, the Stephanie surveillance project would be getting underway in a matter of hours. Right now, I had all I could do to just find the

68

espresso machine and a cigar and get both of them going. Maybe it was drinking with McGovern. Maybe it was dreaming of Kacey. Maybe it was the fact that I hadn't ridden the couch circuit in twenty years and something had sort of thrown me.

An hour later my head was beginning to clear, but as I stood at the window and gazed down at Vandam Street things still seemed to appear a bit funny and unfocused. Quite possibly, I thought, it wasn't really the result of the drinking or the dreaming. It could be that's just the way the world looks when you've got cinnamon oil in your eyes.

16

M Y vision focused clearly at last upon a solitary figure striding down the sidewalk in my direction. The figure was eccentrically and lavishly costumed in a getup extreme even for New York. It had to be either Ratso, or some kind of gay messiah consisting of all the former Village People who'd gone to Jesus returning incarnate in one human form. When it stopped under my window and began shrieking like a loon, I realized the messiah had not returned. Ratso, however, most decidedly had.

The cat joined me at the window and peered down in disgust. Even by Ratso standards this outfit was outlandish. The full-length raccoon fur coat was terribly out of fashion—and out of favor—these days, and the sparkling, brightly striped biblical-style burnoose did little to ingratiate the eye of the beholder. Add to this hideous combination Professor Henry Hill band-leader pants, D'Artagnan leather gauntlets, red, white, and blue chaps, mirrored sunglasses, black studded biker gloves, and canary yellow cowboy boots. Over his shoulder Ratso carried a big burlap bag containing God knows what and which gave him the rather remarkable appearance of an urban, dysfunctional Johnny Appleseed.

I went to the mantelpiece like a man in a dream, plucked the smiling puppet head from its perch, and walked back and raised the window. I flipped poor Yorick into the chill late afternoon sky and watched him glide gracefully into the hands of the madman below. Something was clearly going on in Ratso's mind. In the past his wardrobe had always been unpleasant, but never in all the time I'd known him had it ever been this contrived or elaborate.

"He looks like he's just come from a fashion show at a mental hospital," I said to the cat as I closed the window.

The cat, of course, said nothing. She wouldn't have liked Ratso if she'd found him in the bulrushes wearing nothing but swaddling cloth, and she certainly wasn't going to like him now.

Moments later, Ratso stomped into the loft, flipped me the puppet head, and made his mandatory beeline for the refrigerator, which he opened, surveyed methodically, apparently found nothing, and closed. He turned back to face the room in a state very close to melancholy. He was nothing, however, if not resilient. By the time he'd worked his way over to the espresso machine and drawn himself a cup of the steaming black liquid, his ebullient spirit had returned.

"So are we ready for tonight, Kinkstah?" he said with great enthusiasm.

"What do you mean we?" I said. "You got a mouse in your burnoose?"

"What do you mean, Kinkstah? Spying on Stephanie was *my* idea. Of course I'm going along with you guys."

"Ratso, how did you even know we're doing this surveillance tonight?"

71

"A large Irish leprechaun told me."

"Great."

"You can't leave Watson behind, Sherlock. What do you think I have in the bag?"

"My chances for future happiness?"

"Guess again, Kinkstah!"

"Three hundred and sixty-four pairs of fresh underwear in case the surveillance takes longer than expected?"

"You're gettin' warm, Kinkstah! The bag is full of stuff for disguises."

"Ah, Watson, as always you're prepared for any eventuality! But if the disguises are in the bag, what do you consider you're wearing at the moment?"

"Just some things I threw together," he said.

It looked like something the cat threw up, but I didn't vocalize that sentiment. It would have been wasted. Ratso would certainly not have been offended. Nothing offended Ratso. But it was more than possible that it might've offended the cat. Everything offended the cat. At the moment merely looking at Ratso seemed to be enough to put her off her nice Southern Gourmet Dinner.

Whether Ratso was eccentric and flamboyant, or whether he was certifiably clinically ill was not really a judgment I was qualified to make. All I knew was that in spite of the fact that his outfit was hideously inappropriate for any manner of surveillance operation, I was not about to cast asparagus upon his enthusiasm for the venture. Far better for Ratso to devote his energies to spying on Stephanie than to become further involved in snooping around with the Khadija situation and possibly get us all killed.

"So where's the pink suitcase, Kinkstah?" he asked, realizing my worst fears. Once Ratso got on to something you generally needed a forklift to get him off it.

"Oh, it's lying around somewhere."

"You mean the girl never bothered to pick it up? That's pretty strange, Kinkstah."

"Oh, I don't know. It probably happens more than we think."

"Not unless she's dead or there's something in the suitcase too hot for her to pick up."

"Ah, Watson, what a joy it is that you yet retain your sense of the melodramatic!"

"Ah, Sherlock, then I perceive that you did open the suitcase?"

"Ah, Watson, must there be never a nuance that escapes that ever-vigilant mind of yours?"

"So what the fuck was in the suitcase?" shouted Ratso.

There was no way in hell I was going to tell Ratso. It'd be about as prudent as becoming pen pals with John Hinckley. I casually lopped the butt off a cigar and carefully set fire to the tip with a kitchen match.

"Just some things she threw together," I said.

17

A F T E R convincing Ratso to jettison some of the more ludicrous items of his sartorial arsenal, the two of us set out together for Chinatown. He'd finally stopped prattling on about the suitcase and instead, thankfully, was focusing his tedium on the imminent Stephanie DuPont surveillance caper. It was now just goosing five-thirty and Rambam and McGovern were set to meet at the loft a little before eight. That left plenty of time for me to meditate on just how excited Rambam would be when he realized that the fourth member of our little spy ring was going to be Ratso.

I began having some second thoughts myself about the wisdom of having any human interaction with Ratso shortly after a hearty meal at Big Wong's Restaurant on Mott Street. We were walking through Chinatown belching like Eskimos when Ratso, almost as if in a state of clinical recall, began badgering me once again about the whereabouts of the suitcase. I had to admit that Ratso was nothing if not persistent. My problem was that he was beginning to wear me down. Unfortunately, the only secrets I'd ever actually managed to keep were the ones I'd forgotten.

"Ratso," I said, "I'm begging you to stop. I'm telling you this for your own good. There isn't a suitcase. There never was a suitcase. You only imagined that there was a suitcase."

"Even though I may not be able to see the suitcase," said Ratso, "I know there is one."

"Therefore you think the suitcase is the one true God."

"No," said Ratso, as he bummed a cigar, "but I have accepted the toilet kit as my own personal savior."

"Ratso, for God's sake, forget it. Put these things out of your mind. There is no suitcase. There is no toilet kit."

"What's really bothering me at the moment," said Ratso, gazing down the crowded corridor of Canal Street, "is that there is no toilet."

About twenty minutes later, after hopping a hack for Hudson Street and hooking a left at Vandam, Ratso was safely ensconced in the rain room of the loft taking a Nixon maybe four feet away from the hidden cache of passports buried in the cat litter. It really was the perfect location, I thought, as I puffed a cigar by the window and waited for the espresso machine to perform. If a nosey parker like Ratso could take a Nixon that close to the goods and not suspect anything, I doubted if a cadre of terrorists or a phalanx of State Department agents would ever tumble to my secret hiding place either. The only one who possibly might discover the passports was the cat, and there was very little likelihood of that since she'd taken to vindictively dumping in various locations around the loft lately, hardly ever going near the cat litter. This behavior on her part was really quite understandable and almost never bothered the Kinkster. It was a big loft and it was a free country, and when you change the cat litter once every seven years whether it needs it or not you have to expect certain ramifications, not to mention certain defecations to result from your actions or lack thereof. Furthermore, there was a rather sensitive balance between man and nature in the loft, and it wasn't something I was especially eager to tinker with.

It was seven-forty-five when the two red telephones on my desk began to ring. Ratso was busily sorting through the ridiculous contents of his laundry bag, looking for all the world like a large, rather unpleasant child getting ready to leave for camp. I was busily sorting through all the things I might not want to know about Stephanie DuPont that I could be about to find out. I picked up the blower on the left.

"Take-It-Easy Trailer Park," I said.

"That's what you think," said Rambam. "We should be there to get you in about ten minutes. You sure you're ready for this?"

"I guess so. I've just about reached the point where I don't really give a damn about anything."

"That's the spirit."

"By the way, how'd it go with the young Israeli aerobics instructor last night?"

"Not too well. She turned into a middle-aged Latvian computer programmer. Now what about the subject of tonight's little operation? Can you verify for the chief field investigator and the head reporter on the scene—that's you, McGovern—"

"Well, fuck me dead, mate—"

"I repeat—can you verify for us that the subject is at home?"

"How would I do that?"

"There's an old investigative technique that may be applicable in this situation. You dial her phone number. If she answers, you hang up."

"Sounds kind of pubescent."

"What else is there?"

Feeling like a fourteen-year-old, I cradled the blower, then scooped it up again, and punched out Stephanie's number. It rang a few times and then her familiar, sweet-and-sour, if slightly-too-expectant voice came on the line. Obviously, I wasn't whom she expected to hear from and, of course, she didn't. I cradled the blower again, relieved at least that Ratso was still absorbed in inventorying his sick disguises.

About ten minutes later I was in full battle gear—cowboy hat, Oliver Twist hand-me-down overcoat, and three cigars for the road—and pacing back and forth in the kitchen when the phones rang.

"That'll be Rambam," I said.

"I'm ready, Kinkstah!" shouted Ratso, as he threw the laundry bag over his shoulder like a strange, Semitic Santa Claus.

"I still think you should stay here, Watson," I said.

"It was my fucking idea!" he shouted.

"What took you so long?" said Rambam, when I'd effectively collared the blower.

"I was adjusting the satellite dish on my head," I said. "Where are you?"

"I'm parked up the block. The subject was at home I take it?"

"Correct."

"If she's got a date with the perpetrator she'll be coming out fairly soon. Either he'll be picking her up or she'll leave alone and rendezvous with him. We'll tail the subject to the rendezvous site and set up field operations then."

"I'm with you, Sub-commander Marcos."

"Subject may be moving quickly so you'd better get down here. Our vehicle has tinted windows all around so you won't see me or McGovern. We're in a dark van halfway up the block on your side of the street. Go to the window now and make sure you can see us."

"Hang fire."

I put the blower down on the desk and walked to the window to have a look. Ratso, his curiosity now having reached a fevered pitch, unconsciously shadowed my every move. I craned my neck severely to the left but failed to distinguish the surveillance vehicle. I shrugged at Ratso. He shrugged at the cat. The cat sat on the counter and appeared immensely disinterested.

"Where the hell are you guys?" I said, as I collared the blower. "The only thing parked on our side of the street is an old black van with white graffiti scrawled all over it and a six-foot-long cockroach mounted on the top."

"Wait'll you see what it can do with its antennae," said Rambam.

18

CERTAINLY Rambam had seen Ratso trailing along next to me on the sidewalk. Very possibly he'd suspected that I would then climb into the van, and Ratso would toddle on home to his cluttered apartment containing a stuffed polar bear's head, a life-size statue of the Virgin Mary, and over ten thousand books all pertaining in some way or another to the lives of Bob Dylan, Hitler, or Jesus Christ. If that indeed was what Rambam had suspected would happen, it didn't. Ratso and his bulging laundry bag clambered into the van right after me and shut the sliding door firmly behind his large, luminous buttocks.

Rambam was seated behind the wheel of the rather unique-looking vehicle, gazing intently through a pair of binoculars at the entrance to 199B Vandam Street, so he missed Ratso's entry into the side of the van. He also missed Ratso shaking hands with McGovern and, in the process, knocking over what appeared to be a delicately balanced tripod device. To his credit, however, Rambam responded to the situation with civility, maturity, and self-control.

"Out of the van, asshole," he said to Ratso, "before I take this tripod and shove it up your ass!"

"There's a latent homosexual threat if I ever heard one," responded Ratso coolly.

"You can tell that to your therapist," said Rambam, "when he asks you why you've walked around for most of your adult life with a tripod up your ass. Out of the fucking van!"

"Can I quote you on that?" said McGovern, busily taking copious notes in his little investigative reporter's notebook.

"This was *my* fucking idea!" shouted Ratso, standing his ground in the face of an advancing Rambam. "Tell him, Kinkstah!"

"Hold the weddin'!" I said. "Don't put me in the middle of this shit—"

"The maximum allowable personnel for surveillance," intoned Rambam, like a somewhat stressed adult lecturing children in a schoolyard, "is *two*."

"What was that number?" asked McGovern, pen poised over pad, winking broadly at me.

"In this case," Rambam continued, "Kinky and I are conducting the surveillance and McGovern is documenting the effectiveness of various new equipment and procedures—"

"The Shadow knows," said McGovern.

"But to bring into the operation," said Rambam, "a perfectly useless excuse for a human being—"

"Holy shit!" said McGovern. "Look at that!"

The conversation, such as it was, drew to a screeching halt inside the van as a sleek black limo glided gracefully to a stop directly in front of 199B Vandam Street. Out of the limo stepped a tall, dark-headed, confident-looking young man, handsome, I suppose, after a South-of-France type of fashion. While the limo waited, he strode up to the front door of the building and opened

80

it with a key he already had in his possession. He did not, I observed, need anyone to throw him a puppet head.

Sometime later, night was descending upon the city and still the empty limo remained in front of the building. It might've been ten minutes. It might've been fifteen. I waited with the patience some religious sects exhibit as they wait for the world to end. It didn't, of course. It just got darker outside, colder in the van, and darker and colder in my mind as I imagined the handsome young stranger and Stephanie DuPont alone together in her loft.

"What the hell are they doing up there?" I said at last. "What the hell could be taking so long?"

"Maybe they're discussing what restaurant they want to go to," said McGovern.

"Maybe they're having some hors d'oeuvres before they have some hors d'oeuvres," said Ratso.

"Maybe I should've let Rambam shove that tripod up your ass," I said.

"Maybe I should've never shared my idea with you," said Ratso.

"Yeah, well maybe we should all share a moment of silence," said Rambam. "They're coming out of the building."

There is something about the facile happiness of beautiful young couples that is inherently irritating to the mind of the rugged individualist. There do seem to be many beautiful young couples in this world and very few individualists left, rugged or otherwise. Most of them, like Van Gogh or Anne Frank, have died lonely deaths, having made only a few, clumsy, adolescent, star-crossed, interpersonal steps toward love before they got run over by trains passing in the night. It wasn't spiritually best foot forward, I thought, to watch too many happy young couples get into limousines. Nothing against limousines, of course. They can't help it if they're sleek, and even if you die in the gutter, they'll sometimes take you to the bone orchard. I wanted to warn Stephanie DuPont about walking on Agamemnon's blood red carpet. I wanted to take her hand and save her from this stranger and this limo. There is so little human grace in the act of watching a happy young couple getting into a limo. There is more grace and more humanity released in this world when you listen to two whippoorwills calling each other in the dark.

"Too bad it's a limo," I said, as we watched the happy young couple climb into the limo. "I've been cruelly denied the chance to say: 'Follow that cab.'"

"It's much easier to follow a limo," said Rambam as he started the ignition. "This is not, of course, the vehicle of choice for *tailing* a limo."

"This is not the vehicle of choice for tailing a pogo stick with a rearview mirror," I said.

"Then why are we riding in this ridiculous-looking van with a giant cockroach on top?" said Ratso.

"The cockroach belongs," said Rambam. "You're the insect in this soup. But to answer your stupid question, this is not only a state-of-the-art mobile surveillance headquarters, but it's also, if used very sparingly, the kind of setup that the subject would never in a million years lamp to. He'd have to ask himself: 'What kind of moronic assholes would be crazy enough to try to spy on me in that piece of shit van with the giant fucking cockroach on top?'"

"Can I quote you on that?" asked McGovern.

"That's off the record," said Rambam.

"So's the precise nature of the investigation," I added.

"Understood," said McGovern, as Rambam hurtled the van through an alley, keeping the limo just in sight. "This is strictly an account of how Rambam operates his high-tech spy toys and their effectiveness in the field."

"Should make for riveting reading," said Ratso.

"I'll rivet your scrotum to the roof," said Rambam to Ratso, as he hooked a sharp, rattling left turn. "You can ride with the cockroach."

"No," I said. "That might make us too conspicuous."

"That chauffeur must be a NASCAR driver," said Rambam, as he barreled along a little closer to the limo than I'd have liked. "Just wait'll you see this fucking cockroach go into action."

"Can I quote you on that?" asked McGovern.

"Off the record," said Rambam.

After getting stuck in traffic for a while, situated several cars behind the limo, and after more exchanges of lighthearted banter between Ratso and Rambam, we followed the subjects onto a trendy, tree-lined street nestled somewhere in the circuitous heart of the West Village. The limo pulled up in front of a rather precious, coochi-poochi-boomalini restaurant, and the driver got out, walked around to the curbside rear door in a hurried yet dignified fashion, and the happy couple got out and moved quickly out of sight into the restaurant. Rambam put the pest control van into overdrive and performed a decidedly illegal U-turn which eventually landed us on the far side of the street with a fairly good view of the place, not that there was a hell of a lot to see. The van continued to crawl slowly along the curb, attempting to find the perfect angle on the little restaurant. With the city by now thoroughly cloaked in darkness, I was beginning to wonder about the efficacy of Rambam's night vision device. Well, we'd soon see, I thought, or, very possibly, we wouldn't.

Rambam finally brought the distasteful-looking vehicle to a full stop immediately in back of a red Porsche with a vanity license plate that read: UNWED MD.

"There but for fortune," said Rambam.

19

I T started to rain just as Rambam began to assemble the night vision device on a tripod inside the narrow confines of the van. At approximately the same time, barely three feet away from this rather sensitive operation, Ratso was rummaging through his laundry bag of disguises with what seemed like an increasing degree of frustration.

"I can't find my Hari Krishna outfit," he confided at last, to no one in particular.

"What a fucking shame," said Rambam, not taking his eye away from the small telescopelike device mounted on the tripod.

"This may be a stupid question," said McGovern from the front of the van, "but what would you do with the Hari Krishna outfit if you found it?"

"These are *disguises,* McGovern," said Ratso, like a social worker talking to a slow client. "Sherlock here will be the first to tell you that the subject of our surveillance tonight is quite familiar with all of our physical appearances—"

"That's why she's in there with the guy from France," said Rambam.

"It seems quite obvious to me," Ratso continued obliviously, "that if it were to become necessary for one of us to go out into the field, that person would require a disguise of some sort."

"That's positively visionary, Watson!" I exclaimed. "As always, you're at least ten steps ahead of the criminal mind."

"Unfortunately, we're not dealing with criminals," said Rambam. "We're dealing with two young people out on a date."

Rambam continued to make minute adjustments on the night vision device. Ratso continued to wade through his traveling warehouse of disguises. McGovern continued to make copious notes in his little notebook, which looked ridiculously small because he was such a large man. I lit up a cigar and watched the rain through the tinted, one-way windows of the van. The view outside looked more dense and opaque than a foggy night on Baker Street.

"Is the rain creating any problem with the night vision device?" asked McGovern.

"No," said Rambam, "it's only creating a problem by keeping the four of us cooped up together in this van."

"Could turn into a *Lord of the Flies* situation," I said.

"As in 'Kill the pig'?" said Rambam, staring intently at Ratso.

"Before you act out any of your latent homosexual fantasies," said Ratso, blind to danger as well as insult, "why don't you finish your foreplay with that dingus on the tripod?"

"Before you continue shooting your mouth off like a total idiot," said Rambam, standing aside with a theatrical flourish, "why don't you come over here and have a look?"

Rambam moved farther back as Ratso got up and walked over to the device on the tripod. I smoked my cigar as coolly as possible under the circumstances and continued to watch the rain. Ratso peered cautiously through the night vision device.

"Jesus Christ!" he shouted with the prurient enthusiasm of a porn film patron. "I don't fucking believe I'm seeing this!"

"Can I quote you on that?" said McGovern.

"But why is everything so green?" asked Ratso, still firmly glued to the device.

"Not as green as Kinky's going to be when he takes a look," said Rambam.

Even if you love the rain, there are times in your life when it's going to let you down. When everything you thought you believed in floats away like a paper boat upon the sea. Like passive cigar smoke floating upward to the impassive sky filtered through the nuts and bolts and fissures of a rusty tin can van that contains your soul. In my unconscious reticence to see what I really didn't want to see, I was possibly a bit tardy moving up to the tripod. By the time I got there I noticed the large form of McGovern hovering eagerly over the device.

"What're they doin' now?" asked Ratso in a fever of excitement.

"Jesus, Joseph, and Mary!" said McGovern. "This is incredible!"

"What're they doin' now?" repeated Ratso with an almost palpably increasing intensity.

"They're probably doing a little bit more of whatever they were doing before," I said rather irritably. "How much could they possibly be doing sitting at a public bar anyway?"

"You'd be surprised," said Rambam.

It was no easy matter for McGovern to maneuver his large body through the narrow, crowded corridor of the van, but eventually he managed to do just that. The device on top of the tripod lay waiting for me, almost beckoning, like the instrument of the night that it certainly was. Outwardly, I maintained a calm, cavalier air of fatalism. Inwardly, I felt like a small child placing a dreamy lullaby eye upon the viewfinder of his first kaleidoscope. But when I did, all I saw was a blurry field of green.

"They're not there anymore," I said, feeling surprised, relieved, and disappointed all at the same time. "Unless they're hosing on top of the bar under a large undulating green blanket."

"Shit," said Rambam. "They've probably gone to their table in the restaurant."

"Why can't we aim the night vision device into the restaurant?" asked Ratso.

"Because, Captain Nemo," said Rambam, "it only can see through the darkness. It can't see through a brick fucking wall."

"So what do we do now?" asked Ratso.

"Now?" said Rambam. "Let's see if you can find that Hari Krishna outfit."

20

PUTTING a man in the field can often be risky, especially if it's Ratso. But in a fairly ridiculous turn of events, that was precisely what we were forced to do. I was much too familiar to the subject to go into the restaurant undercover. McGovern was too large a candidate even if you'd covered him with a circus tent. Rambam had to stay in mission control and man the equipment, which now included a device called "the ear," a satellite dish that took up about half of the room in the van, and the pen mike that Rambam had apparently used quite successfully while interviewing Nazis in Canada.

"I'm not sure," said McGovern, as Ratso prepared to leave the van, "that a Hari Krishna would wear a T-shirt that reads: 'Jesus Is Coming—Look Busy!'"

"Tough shit," said Ratso, adjusting the plastic, almost entirely shaved head covering as he stepped out into the rain. "It's the only shirt I could find with a religious theme. Besides, with the bright robes and scarves and the tambourine it won't be noticed."

"You can say that again," said Rambam. "Just remember. The ballpoint pen contains a very powerful miniature microphone. Your assignment is to unobtrusively place the pen as close to the subjects as possible."

"Ratso's never done anything unobtrusively in his entire life," I said.

"Wish me luck!" shouted Ratso, giving the tambourine a few trial shakes as he headed out into the rain.

"This could get pretty unpleasant," I said.

"It already *is* pretty unpleasant," said Rambam, as he thoughtfully provided headphones for McGovern and myself. "Dealing with Ratso's always unpleasant, but at least on this occasion we've found a use for him. If he can get the pen mike on the table or even on a chair by the table or even under the table before somebody *hits* him with a table, we're in business."

I did not expect to really hear anything too earth-shattering from "the ear." In truth, after seeing nothing but a waving field of green through the NVD after listening to Ratso, McGovern, and Rambam ejaculate excitedly about what *they'd* witnessed, I was beginning to have some creeping doubts about this whole venture. Maybe the entire thing was a put-on, merely a prank to pay me back for the *Spanking Watson* episode. In fact, I was hoping that the whole thing was a prank, but events immediately subsequent to these reflections proved rather conclusively otherwise. There remained only one mitigating possibility, I thought as I put on the headphones, and it was that life is a prank.

"What the hell is that?" shouted McGovern, rapidly removing the headphones.

"You mean the thing that sounds like a large Chinese dinner gong going off at rapid intervals in the middle of your brain?" I asked. "Those're probably the Tibetan thumb cymbals Allen Ginsberg gave Ratso on the Bob Dylan Tour of 1976."

"I doubt if Ginsberg advised Ratso to meditate while holding a pen mike in the same hand as the cymbals," said Rambam.

"Whatever Ginsberg advised him then," said McGovern, "I'm sure Allen doesn't care now."

"Of course he doesn't," said Rambam. "He's not listening through these goddamn headphones."

Precisely after this little exchange, almost as if Allen Ginsberg had been listening somewhere in a fun corner of the sky, the thumb cymbals fell suddenly silent and we could clearly hear in the headphones the intimate ambience of the little café. People who'd been born with silver spoons in their mouths were clanking those spoons against the silver fillings that had been necessary because they'd eaten too much pâté from some poor goose that some sick Frenchman had hung upside-down for its entire life, and now Allen Ginsberg was in heaven laughing rather loudly because he'd always believed in reincarnation and he knew that soon the goose would come back as the frog and the frog would come back as the goose and the guy with the silver spoon in his mouth would probably be sitting obliviously in this same restaurant for all eternity waiting for his order. Somewhere in the background Sinatra was singing "New York, New York." He was dead, too, but still more alive than the frog or the goose or the guy with the spoon and the fillings. In fact he was probably swinging on a star right now, exchanging phone numbers and hobbies with Allen Ginsberg. Suddenly a loud chanting sound buried Sinatra and practically everything else.

"HARI KRISHNA! HARI KRISHNA! KRISHNA KRISHNA! HARI HARI!"

"Say what?" said Rambam.

"The only Hari Krishna I ever heard," I said, "with a Brooklyn accent."

"We don't claim him," said Rambam. "Try Queens."

"Whatever it is," said McGovern, taking off his earphones again, "it sounds terrible."

"HARI RAMA!" Ratso continued. "HARI RAMA! RAMA RAMA! HARI HARI!"

"If Ginsberg taught him that, then it's a sin against Creation," said Rambam disgustedly.

"Don't blame Ginsberg," I said. "Ratso's self-taught in the Hari Krishna department. I just hope he unloads that microphone before they fat-arm him out of there."

"I lose more pen mikes this way," complained Rambam.

"HARI KRISHNA!" blared Ratso. "HARI KRISHNA! KRISH-NA KRISHNA! HARI HARI!"

In my mind I had an ugly but humorous little picture of Ratso dancing like a shaman in New Guinea on autopilot through the trendy little bistro, the startled diners looking up in horror from their white wines and lobster salads. From all reports Stephanie probably wouldn't be giving him a second glance. She was too wrapped up in her friend from the South of France. That was good, I supposed. It'd really be humiliating if she'd recognized Ratso and lamped to the fact that I was spying on her. But these are the chances one takes when one plows the investigative field. It was appearing less likely by the minute, of course, that I'd ever be plowing Stephanie.

Suddenly, into the sound of mindless chanting was intruded the additional noise of a swiftly developing scuffle. Amidst the sounds of a definite struggle including various crashing noises, the chanting now emerged through the headphones something like this: "HARI RAMA! HARI RAMA! TAKE YOUR FUCK-ING HANDS OFF OF ME!"

A mere moment later Ratso was unceremoniously cartwheeled out the front door of the place into the rain. He picked himself up off the sidewalk, gave a brief, grudging thumbs-up in the direction of the van, and began slowly working his wounded way back toward us. Finally, he climbed into the van to light applause from his fellow surveillance agents.

"That's no fucking way to treat a Hari Krishna," he grumbled as he discarded his wet, ridiculous outfit.

"Did you get the pen mike in position?" Rambam wanted to know.

"I slid it toward their table at the very last moment," said Ratso. "Whether it'll pick up their conversation I couldn't tell you."

"We're about to find out," said Rambam, putting the earphones back on his head.

The rest of us followed suit. We heard the tinkling of glasses and silverware again, muffled conversation, and Keely Smith singing "That Old Black Magic." Then we heard the clear voice of a man with a strong European accent of some kind.

"That crazy guy seemed to be fascinated with you, Stephanie," said the voice.

"Who wouldn't be?" said Stephanie.

"But he seemed almost to know you."

"Maybe I ran into him at an airport somewhere."

"More wine, darling?"

In many respects the situation seemed to me to be just about as close as you could get to waking up in hell next to Oscar Wilde. I might never know for sure what my fellow spies had seen through the NVD, but now I could hear with my own ears precisely how intimate Stephanie's relationship was with this mysterious friend of hers.

"More wine, darling?" mimicked Ratso. "This guy sounds like a fucking nerd, Kinkstah."

"I doubt if he'll be much competition for you, Kink," said McGovern, a bit too patronizingly, I thought.

92

"If he's a fucking nerd and no competition," said Rambam reasonably, "why is he in there and you're out here in the rain in a surveillance van with a cockroach on top?"

"I was wondering about that myself," I said.

I didn't, however, get to wonder about it much longer. More conversation was now coming through the headphones.

"How about stopping by the hotel tonight, bella?" said the suave male voice.

"Can't," said Stephanie. "I take a dance class from the woman across the hall."

"Who happens to be a bush pilot," finished Rambam.

"Then tomorrow night, bella?" continued the man. "Come to my suite at the Carlyle and see the precious little Renoir I bought in Paris last week."

"That's the first time I've ever heard a penis referred to as a Renoir," said McGovern.

"Do we go to the Carlyle tomorrow night?" asked Ratso.

"Up to Kinky," said Rambam.

I was just weighing the joys of eavesdropping upon even more intimate circumstances when a crackling, ear-splitting, splatting sound came over the headphones and the system went dead. We all removed our earphones and looked to Rambam for an explanation. He merely shook his head in disgust.

"What happened?" asked McGovern.

"What do you think happened?" said Rambam gruffly. "A fucking waiter stepped on the pen mike."

"But we got what we needed!" shouted Ratso excitedly. "Tomorrow night, Kinkstah! The Carlyle!"

"I lose more pen mikes this way," said Rambam again.

Later that evening, after Rambam had dropped me off at the loft, I was almost feeling pretty good. Because of a healthy negative attitude I carry toward the world in general, I'd expected to be shocked, surprised, or disappointed, but none of these were the case. Possibly, the sheer thrill of spying upon other human beings was part of it. Possibly, I'd matured to the point where I'd realized that Stephanie was a big girl and could do what she damned well pleased. There was a clear distinction between love and life. Love was blind, and life was its seeing-eye dog—more kind, more beautiful, more human than love itself could ever be. The kind leading the blind. Yet without love there was no one to lead across the street.

It wasn't until sometime later that I'd gotten my first real shock of the night. It was a bewildering, frightening sensation that felt almost like a platonic rape and caused the little hairs on the back of my neck to stand to attention like soldiers who were about to die. It was a little thing, really. I'd noticed it when I'd opened the closet door in the bedroom to put away my coat.

The little pink suitcase was gone.

21

T H E only thing that really differentiates Texas from any other place in the world is the proclivity of its people to urinate out of doors and to attach a certain amount of importance to this popular pastime. Urinating outside goes much further than merely meeting the criterion of what is socially acceptable; it is the way of our people. To walk out under the Texas stars and bleed your lizard is considered the most sacred inalienable right of all citizens of the Lone Star State. Everyone pretty much accepts this in Texas, and if you're urinating outside and a stranger comes upon you—not sexually, of course—they'll by and large leave you alone. If you're urinating say, on the shoulder of a highway, passersby may be seen to nod their approval, some even honking encouragement from their vehicles. This is yet another reason why, when I'm elected the first Jewish governor of Texas, I plan to reduce the speed limits to 54.95.

If you try to urinate outside in New York City, men will come and take you to a mental hospital where you'll be placed before a battery of ball-less wonders called shrinks, psychologists, and social workers, all of whom believe that urinating outdoors is a sure sign of mental illness and just about the sickest thing you can do. Who needs to hear all this psychobabble from these repressed, pointy-headed intellectual nerds anyway? Piss on 'em. I believe that urinating outdoors represents a certain freedom of expression and is a sure sign of mental health and it's not the sickest thing you can do in New York. The sickest thing you can do in New York is to spread cream cheese on one side of a bagel and jelly on the other. Even the shrinks, psychologists, and social workers would probably admit that that's pretty sick, unless of course you urinate on top of the bagel and call it performance art, in which case the battery of ball-less wonders will find you a free-thinking, creative spirit and discuss the matter glowingly, write about the case extensively, compare data for about thirty-seven years, and finally procure for you a federal grant by which time you'll probably be wearing a catheter or have been bugled to Jesus and you damn sure better not try to piss on His parade.

If you have the ill luck to attempt outdoor urination in Nashville, there is a high likelihood that a law enforcement officer may try to shoot your dick. This actually happened to me one lazy afternoon in the late sixties when I was urinating off Billy Swan's fifth-floor balcony at 1909 Broadway just off Music Row. I do recall that LBJ was president at the time and also, as a matter of spiritual trivia, though not necessarily relevant here, that his favorite song reportedly was "Raindrops Keep Fallin' on My Head." At any rate, in kind of a wholesome degenerate Kristofferson country music mood, I was whizzing off Billy Swan's balcony that afternoon when a cop pulled up out of nowhere, got out of the squad car, pulled a gun, and drew a bead on my unprotesting penis. I quickly pulled said penis back into my pants but it was too late. Though I hadn't pissed on a bagel or LBJ's head, the damage, apparently, was done. I was hauled in by the Metro for killin' time and pain with the Singin' Brakeman screamin' through my veins.

On the way down to the cop shop, I paraphrased one of Gustave Flaubert's final sentiments to the two gendarmes who were taking me in. "I only hope that before I die," I quoted, "I shall be able to dump several more buckets of shit upon my fellow man." The cops were not impressed. "They call that literature," I added.

The two cops looked at each other. "What you did ain't literature," said the cop behind the wheel who vaguely resembled Porter Waggoner. "We call it indecent exposure."

In the back seat, wearing bracelets, I wearily watched Music Row slide by outside my window. "Any exposure is good exposure," I said.

I was only at the cop shop for a couple of hours, but it was long enough to see a woman who probably would've been my wife if she hadn't've kept marrying shoe salesmen. Joan of Arc arrested for shop-lifting in a cry for help to her husband who eventually bailed her out and, like everybody else in the world, vaguely resembled Garth Brooks, though, at the time, Garth Brooks vaguely resembled the Baby Jesus.

Now if you try to urinate outdoors in California, George Michael will probably cut your dick off and take it to a cigar bar in Beverly Hills. Any way you cut it, it's better to be pissing your life away in Texas than getting peckertracks waiting for death to come knocking at your door in New York. At one o'clock in the morning with twelve million people all around you, you're all alone wondering whether it will be the State Department coming for you—not sexually—or the terrorists, and the only thing you're sure of is that whoever it is, they're going to be highly agitato. A little pink suitcase without any passports is not what they wanted for Christmas.

You walk over to the cat litter box in the rain room. Nothing's changed. Everything's in the same position. Just like the rest of the world, the dry turds are still on top.

You walk over to the blower and call Rambam in Brooklyn. "The little pink suitcase is gone," you tell him.

Like all people in Brooklyn who get awakened in the middle of the night, he shouts loud enough to hear him in Manhattan without the blower. "Whatta ya mean the little pink suitcase is gone?"

"Just what I said," you say. "The little pink suitcase is gone."

"Then you better be, too," he says.

You hate to leave the cat to fend for herself, but you got to. If anybody harms that cat, you think, you'll become a terrorist yourself or maybe join the State Department or maybe one's the same thing as the other. You put on your hat and coat and grab a handful of cigars for the road and leave the cat in charge of a job you wouldn't give to a dog.

As you walk through a light rain to Ratso's place in SoHo, you don't have time to feel guilty. You don't even have time to take a leak along the way. Besides, you might get arrested by Porter Waggoner. A social worker might come and take away your childhood. You might see an angel sleeping in a doorway or your dead lover weeping in the park. You might be tempted to shed a tear or two yourself for every stray soul crossing the universe or every stray cat crossing a discarded chest of drawers. If you do, just remember what my dear dead friend Tim Mayer once told me: "We weep for ourselves, Kinkster."

22

BECAUSE of Ratso's driving, almost clinically ill curiosity, and my own almost pathological inability to keep anything under my cowboy hat for more than the life span of the mayfly, I'd soon revealed to Ratso the entire tale of the terrorists and the State Department, along with my concern for the welfare of the cat, because I fully expected someone to return to my loft soon on a scavenger hunt for missing passports. Like a small child listening to a bedtime story and interrupting often for additional details, Ratso absorbed the whole sordid megillah as I at last unbosomed myself of the data of life or death from the supine vantage point of Ratso's decrepit, degenerate, skid-marked couch. As I unfolded the narrative, the story seemed pretty wiggy even to me.

"There's a few things that don't add up," said Ratso, just as I was almost drifting off to sleep for the first time in two hundred years.

"There's a lot of things that don't add up," I said irritably.

"Life. Love. Why this apartment looks precisely the same as when I first crashed here over twenty years ago. Why, in all that time, you haven't bought a new couch."

"First of all," said Ratso in a soft, patient, rational voice that had been festering somewhere in his background of psychology, "this whole mystery seems to hinge on this Khadija woman. Just from your brief encounter with her on the plane, you cared about her enough to bring her baggage home with you. Whether she's an innocent girl or a terrorist, you seemed to have believed in her in some way. The suitcase was very securely locked and she had no reason to think you would or could open it. She knew where you lived. Why is she playing such a coy and furtive game with you, Kinkstah? She's already met you on the plane and she's called and made a date to get together with you. What happened in her life after that? Why didn't she come back?"

"Why doesn't Jesus come back?" I said.

"Jesus doesn't have an American passport?"

"Try again."

"Jesus didn't leave a vibrator in his suitcase?"

"Watson, your mind is working feverishly. It's such a pleasure to be trapped here in your squalid flat listening at gunpoint to you masturbating tiny baby chipmunks."

"So what do you plan to do, Sherlock? Sublet my couch for the winter?"

"As tempting a notion as that is, nevertheless it shall not stand. I shall return to the loft and you, Watson, shall return with me."

"To check for clues, Sherlock?"

"To check on the cat. No good terrorist or revolutionary would ever harm a cat, but I'm not so sure about the State Department."

"And then we'll check for clues?"

"Then we'll check your brain into a high school science exhibit," I said curtly. "Sorry, Watson. I'm somewhat distracted just now."

"Clues," said Ratso, ever oblivious to insult. "Clues as to who stole the suitcase from your closet."

"Wonderful, Watson. You never lose the scent. By the way, there appears to be the odor of rotting meat in this apartment. I haven't smelled anything in ten years thanks to incessant cigar smoking and the previous recreational use of Peruvian marching powder, but it would seem I'm picking up a definite olfactory signal."

"Old corned beef sandwich, Sherlock. In the trash in the kitchen. Goes out with the next garbage pickup."

"And when would that be, Watson?"

"About the time Jesus gets back."

"Ah, Watson, your earthy humor never fails to imbue an investigation with a pathetic veneer of cloying humanity. I will now, against my better judgment, tell you the one clue that is of paramount importance in this case! I say against my better judgment, Watson, because you have a very trusting spirit, and if, God forbid, you should fall into the hands of the terrorists—well, it's better left unsaid."

"So what's the fucking clue?"

"The clue, my dear Watson, is the position of the dried cat turds on top of the litter box."

"You're shittin' me."

"I'm afraid not, Watson. You see, I've hidden the purloined passports under the cat litter in a little cellophane bag that God provided. Tomorrow when we return to the loft, if the dried cat turds on top of the litter box are *not* in their accustomed position, it can mean only one thing."

"What's that, Sherlock?"

"We're fucked."

"But how will we know if the culprits are the terrorists or the State Department?"

"Marvelous, Watson! Can nothing escape your zealous intellectual pursuit?"

Ratso may actually have been blushing. I wasn't quite sure because for about the nineteenth time in the course of the conversation I'd closed my eyes in exhaustion and ennui. It didn't take long, however, for Ratso's rodentlike voice to pipe up again, effectively shish-kebabing any sheep I'd thought about starting to count.

"Sherlock, do I detect a lingering fondness on your part for this mysterious woman, Khadija?"

"Ah Watson," I said, once more opening my eyes, "I thought you'd never ask. Unfortunately, I've been having some problems with interpersonal relations for about fifty-three years now. Sadly, I no longer love, despise, respect, or appreciate anyone for themselves anymore. My heart is like an Easter chick. I've been with so many people that they all start reminding me of each other."

"Then how will we ever know if the State Department or the terrorists stole the suitcase?"

"Quite simple, Watson. If the State Department stole the suitcase they will not return, for they have no way of knowing if anything's missing."

"And if the terrorists stole the suitcase?"

"Just like Jesus," I said, "they'll be coming back and they'll be really pissed."

23

T H E following afternoon, after circumcising our watches with Rambam several hours earlier, the three of us met on the corner of Vodka and Coca-Cola and made our cautious way to Vandam Street. Both Rambam and Ratso were packing—Rambam, a weapon, Ratso, his lunch. The latter individual had been sorely disappointed, apparently, in the grub department of the loft on a number of recent visits. He wasn't taking any chances. I wasn't either.

"Are you sure," I said to Rambam, "that one gun will be enough protection against a gang of terrorists or cadre of State Department agents?"

"Who said I had only one gun?" said Rambam. "On the other hand, if I had fourteen it wouldn't make any difference. If we happen to run into the terrorists up there in your loft, I can tell you right now they're not leaving until they get those passports, even if they have to kill us."

"I don't know, Kinkstah," said Ratso, visibly wavering in enthusiasm as we walked. "Are you sure this is a good idea?"

"How the hell do I know," I said. "You were the one who wanted to look for clues."

"Of course," said Rambam, "if it's the State Department, we won't have that problem. They'd never allow themselves to be caught doing something illegal like breaking and entering. They'd probably post an undercover guy out front with a walkie-talkie and they'd all scamper away before we got near the place. So, given the two choices, I'm rooting for the State Department."

"Me, too," said Ratso in a small voice that noticeably lacked its usual ebullient, rodentlike timbre.

"There's nothing to worry about," I said, with a confidence I didn't feel. "There'll probably be nobody there but the cat, and she'll turn her back on me and sulk because I've been out all night."

"Or we could meet a man named Abu Pinhead," said Rambam, "who's wearing a ski mask and holding an automatic weapon."

"If somebody throws down the puppet head," said Ratso, "I'm not going up."

"As long as somebody doesn't throw down *your* head," said Rambam, "what do you care?"

"Maybe," I said to Ratso, "you should've worn the Hari Krishna outfit that you used so successfully last night. The terrorists wouldn't kill a Hari Krishna, would they?"

"After last night," said Rambam, "any self-respecting Hari Krishna's probably back at the ashram praying to the most holy god of all barnyard animals and asking him why in the hell he let Allen Ginsberg give Ratso those fucking finger cymbals."

"Not to mention that hideous detachable ponytail," I said.

"They're not just finger cymbals," said Ratso, as the loft came into sight. "They're also worn on the thumb. They might more appropriately be referred to as hand cymbals."

"Hand job," said Rambam.

As we cautiously approached 199B Vandam, my home away from home away from home, it became apparent, even to my relatively untrained eye, that no State Department lackey was lurking undercover with a walkie-talkie. The street was so empty and silent, in fact, you could almost hear the garbage trucks daydreaming as they slumbered by the curbside. The trite phrase "too quiet" indeed might've leapt to a lesser mind. I wasn't sure what Rambam or Ratso were thinking, but my own gray matter department was pregnant with possibilities, none of which were very pleasant.

Ratso and I loitered at the deserted doorway while Rambam took a quick reconnaissance stroll around the corner. I puffed a cigar and Ratso opened his sack lunch and took out a large, somewhat wilted-looking bagel, complete with lox, onion, cream cheese, and tomato. He proceeded to begin rather complacently eating the bagel. I had to admire his cool under the circumstances. It's one thing to dress up like a Hari Krishna and scurry forth from a van with a giant cockroach on top to spy upon a beautiful blonde. It's quite another to calmly eat a bagel when you know there's a fairly high probability that terrorists may be lying in wait for you four stories above your poppy seeds.

"How in the hell can you possibly eat at a time like this?" I asked, allowing a hint of irritation born of impatience to creep into my voice.

"I've got to fortify myself," said Ratso rather defensively.

If there was a rational reply to Ratso's statement, I never got the chance to make it. Rambam had rounded the corner and came fairly skipping toward us along the sidewalk.

"Into the valley of death," he said cheerfully, "rode the three Jewboys."

"Any last words?" I asked Ratso.

"Yeah," he said. "Would you mind not smoking while I'm eating."

"Let's get it over with," said Rambam, gesturing toward the locked doors of the building. "There's probably nobody up there anyway."

I got out the key calmly enough and opened the door. The freight elevator was not in the little lobby waiting to welcome us, so Rambam headed up the stairs. I followed him, and Ratso, who blessedly had finished his bagel, brought up the rear. The stairs, like the street, were strangely quiet. Where was a passing lesbian when you needed one?

By the time we'd reached the fourth-floor stairwell, tensions had become stronger and imaginations had become more vivid. Ratso had inquired several times rather nervously about whether or not we were taking the right approach, to which Rambam replied that the elevator hadn't been available, to which Ratso replied that that wasn't what he'd meant. By the time we reached the door to the loft, however, all conversation ceased rather abruptly.

The door was ajar.

24

I ' V E always associated the phrase "A door is ajar" with the death of my mother. It has to do with the 1983 Jesus Christler convertible named Dusty that had once belonged to her, now belongs to me, and often still comments in a well-modulated, Japanese-installed voice: "A door is ajar." It has to do with the right things you think about at the sad times, and Dusty sitting out there all alone in the parking lot of the funeral home with all of the somber, slightly snobbish, nameless luxury vehicles that typically seem to frequent funerals. When the Lord closes the door, he opens a little window. A door is ajar. As you go through life, you'll hold her hand more than you know. I want to hold your hand. The Lord always picks his most beautifulest flowers first. Be with me. A door is ajar. A jar is a door. Praise dog. Ah, Dusty, my mother, my sweetheart, my cat, all in heaven and only you and I driving like hell down a Dusty road somewhere far inside the secret lonely linkage of the heart.

Khadija was sitting on the couch. The cat was sitting on her lap. Both were staring down the short, ugly barrel of Rambam's gun. Neither the cat nor Khadija appeared to be even the slightest bit concerned. The cat merely stood up slowly on Khadija's lap and stretched herself. Khadija stretched her long languorous legs. They were longer, slightly darker, and definitely more sinewy, attractive, and somehow more athletic than I'd remembered when I'd seen her a lifetime ago on the plane. Possibly this was because she was now wearing an extremely short skirt.

"What took you so long, Big Dick?" she said in a soft and sulky voice.

There is no worse feeling, so Rambam confided to me later, than pointing a gun at someone and being totally ignored. Therefore it was only moments after Khadija had made her introductory remark that Rambam pocketed the weapon, checked out the bedroom, the dumper, and the fire escape, and pulled me aside for a brief consultation.

"You know my motto," he said in a Brooklyn whisper. "Never let ideological differences get in the way of a good piece of ass."

"What if it's a trap?" I said.

"Every good piece of ass is a trap," said Rambam.

"Spare me your alarmingly sexist philosophy," I said. "What the hell am I supposed to do?"

"First Ratso and I will leave you two lovebirds alone—that is, once I get his eyes unglued from Khadija's legs. I've seen worse legs, by the way. After we leave, I'll check the perimeter a bit and make sure Abu Pinhead and his cousins are nowhere around. Then you bed the broad or, from the looks of things, the broad beds you. Far be it from me to be a fifth wheel."

"Then what?"

"Then she says: 'You were great. Where's the suitcase?'"

"*Then* what do I say?"

"You feign indignation. You tell her something like this: 'You don't call me for days. You break into my loft. You hose my brains out for two hours. And all you want is your suitcase. You could've just asked me.'"

"Then she'll say: 'I *did* just ask you.' Then what'll I do?"

As Rambam and I were conferring in the kitchen, Ratso had moved in on Khadija and the two of them appeared to be making small talk. Every once in a while she'd look my way with what I had to admit were bedroom eyes. She was certainly a beautiful terrorist. She didn't exactly strike fear into my heart, but she was doing a pretty good job of making me nervous.

"You go to the fucking closet and look for the fucking suitcase," said Rambam, "which, of course, isn't fucking there."

"Then what?"

"You feign shock. You can't believe it. The suitcase is gone."

"I feign this. I feign that. What if she doesn't believe me?"

"Don't worry," said Rambam. "She'll probably be feigning some things herself."

"Yeah? Like what?"

"Like orgasm," said Rambam.

I walked back over and sat down on the couch next to Khadija. I wasn't sure that Rambam's sex-for-suitcase scenario would play out, but it was worth a try. Anything for the home team. I watched Khadija's shining brown eyes and soothing olive skin and sexy red lips. I watched Rambam casually collar Ratso and drag him out of the loft with a big wave and a wicked, rather suggestive smile. Khadija did not seem to notice they'd left until she heard the door close. She'd been too busy, apparently, stroking the cat and staring at me. There was six thousand years of dangerous karma in that gaze. I couldn't afford to blink.

"Alone at last," she said.

25

Y O U may not be aware of this, but it's against the law to transport bull semen on a Greyhound bus in Texas. There are many reasons for this restriction, but first and foremost among them is the fact that it's very difficult to wash bull semen out of a peach-colored dress. Just knowing this information was one thing. Being able to use it effectively in interpersonal relations was quite another. You'd think that a man, a woman, a Greyhound bus, a peach-colored dress, and a gallon or two of bull semen would make for a good country song by Willie Nelson or possibly even a play by Willie Shakespeare. You'd think these disparate elements could cling comfortably, tragically together like colorfully colored cowboy shirts spinning into each other's arms in the dryer of a laundromat at midnight. Unfortunately, there's a fine line between fiction and nonfiction and I think I snorted it in 1979. As events and individuals unfolded, Rambam's lascivious little scenario didn't quite hold up. But it almost did, and that wasn't so bad either.

"Sorry I just dropped in like this," she said, as she sensuously stroked the cat. "The door was open."

"I see. How'd you get in the building?"

"A woman on her way out let me in."

"A passing lesbian, no doubt."

"A what?"

"Just a private joke. So where've you been all my life? I'd given you up for missing in action."

"I've been busy as hell," she said, hiking her skirt up a little farther along those brown sinuous legs that really should've been illegal. "But now it's time to relax and unwind a little. A drink would be nice."

A drink *would* be nice, I thought. My tongue was getting dry looking at her legs.

"A drink would be nice," I agreed, getting up and ankling it over to the kitchen. "What would you like? Whiskey or whiskey?"

"That's a difficult choice," she said, leaning languorously back and pulling one bare brown foot onto the couch so that it nestled enviably directly under a pair of now-and-again-visible shiny pink panties. They must've been fairly new, I figured. If I didn't miss my guess most of her other lingerie was currently residing at the State Department. Some agent had probably locked his door and right at this moment might've been wearing some of her wardrobe on his head.

"Life's full of difficult choices," I said. "That's why there's so many Moonie marriages."

"In that case I'll take whiskey," she said, smiling in an attractive but vaguely sharklike manner.

I poured out two shots on the kitchen counter into a chipped *Imus in the Morning* coffee cup and the trusty old bull's horn. They were two long shots, and they needed to be long. I needed to keep my eyes off the predatory smile and the peripatetic pink panties, and it wasn't the easiest thing in the world to accomplish that little feat. Rambam had been right, I thought. It was a typical terrorist tactic to try to seduce me. I couldn't let it go to my head. All the woman really wanted was her suitcase. The best evidence that this was true was the fact that she hadn't even mentioned the suitcase. On the other hand, I was spiritually horny enough not to be a shrinking violet regardless of the fact that the other party looked like a sexy shark swimming in for the kill. Considering that my social calendar consisted of spying on Stephanie DuPont at the Carlyle Hotel tonight, the shark was looking better all the time. Life was all a game anyway, I figured, and you never stop playing until you die trying.

I walked the two shots over to the davenport and handed the bull's horn to Khadija. Her hand touched mine as she took the bull's horn. It seemed somehow dainty and sinewy at the same time.

"It's considered a great honor to drink from the sacred bull horn," I said.

"Bull horn, bullshit," she said, throwing back the shot, then grabbing my arm and pulling me onto the couch in such a violent fashion as to make me almost spill my drink. "Why are you afraid of me? I thought we had some unfinished business."

It all *is* a game, I thought, and she's playing it to the hilt. Now if I could only keep up my part of it. Keeping it up, of course, was not a terribly difficult problem by this time.

"Speaking of business," I said, "what kind of business are you in?"

"Software," she said, smiling a hard little smile. "I'm really a high-priced errand girl for my brother. He owns the company. We're in so many different countries now I can't even keep track."

I'll bet you can't, I thought. The sense of calculation in her dangerous, lovely head was almost palpable. I wasn't buying any of it, but like everybody else in the world, I played along.

"That must keep you hoppin'."

"Right now," she said, "I'd like you to hop up and get us both another drink. You seem to have spilled most of yours."

She was going to a lot of trouble to get that suitcase, I thought, as I dutifully hopped off the couch and accompanied my monstro-erection over to the bottle of Jameson's. If I'd found myself in this situation under any other circumstances I'd've been happy to let that cute little shark eat me alive. As it was, my ego was struggling with a mild case of suitcase envy. But the red flags were out all along the parade route. And it's not polite, not to mention potentially dangerous, to let a terrorist know that you suspect she's a terrorist. You have to keep playing the game, keep bringing drinks, and keep making small talk or the situation could get ugly. If you thought about it, the whole thing bore some rather uncanny parallels to the *Tales of the Arabian Nights*.

I don't usually kiss on the first date, but I had met Khadija before on the plane from which she had so mysteriously disappeared, so I figured we'd gotten the mandatory handshake out of the way. I'd meant to ask her about her disappearance, but I never got around to it. As late afternoon shadows crossed the loft, the couch, for all the world, had turned into an extremely passionate magic carpet ride. We were literally lost in each other's arms for a time during which I forgot to remember that this broad must've been one hell of a terrorist. Indeed, I kept a glimmer of hope alive that she was an innocent pawn of her brother's. But she didn't kiss like an innocent pawn of any man's.

At one point, as she was lying on top of me and I stared into the brown eternity of her eyes, I truly felt the heat of the desert like a Bedouin on his way to Cairo. I started to reach between

113

her legs to the little shiny patch of pink, but I was quickly re-buffed.

"None of that," she said firmly. "I don't know you well enough."

"Sorry," I said. "My heroin suppository seems to be kicking in."

"But I've got another idea," she said.

Before I knew it I was sitting up blearily on the couch and she was on her knees on the floor between my legs, feverish fingers fumbling for my fly. Soon the situation, if you wanted to call it that, was out of my hands and into the capable hands of Khadija. One of the most beautiful sights in the world is watching your own penis disappear into the mouth of a woman who loves you. That wasn't quite the case here, of course, but she'd been my penis's first passenger in some time now and I wasn't about to throw her off the train.

"Khadija," I said, "you're wonderful."

"Shut up," she said, and kept at it.

The climax of the story seems a little vague even to me at this time. I just remember half closing my eyes and seeing blurry, dissociated images before Khadija finally freed the hostages. Like pieces of a puzzle in an out-of-body experience, I had many irrational subconscious pictures flash briefly across the old-time drive-in-theater screen of my gray matter department. Like life itself, the images were jumbled, mixed-up, insane, and they vanished quickly, signifying zippo and I'm not talking about the lighter. All I can remember is a man in a Greyhound dress, a woman in a peach-colored bus, and the whole world drowning in a biblical deluge, though it was probably only a gallon or two, of something that certainly appeared to be bull semen.

26

W H E N she learned that the suitcase was missing, Khadija was not a happy terrorist. I did my best to feign shock and surprise as I stood at the door of the violated closet and ejaculated appropriate phrases of figurative bull semen, but I'm not sure I completely brought it off. It was an interesting little chess game, however. My position was that I was totally confounded by the disappearance of the suitcase while making no mention, of course, as to the nature of its contents. Her position was one of displaying a sort of controlled irritation over the lost baggage but not wanting to push it far enough so as to make me overly curious as to what might've been inside. The war of wills quickly devolved from a game of chess to a poker game in which both of us were obviously bluffing.

The erstwhile passionate couple seemed somewhat starcrossed by the time we said our rather curt farewells, and Khadija blew out of the loft like a sandstorm in the Sahara. Before she left we'd both said all the right things about the suitcase that had come between us. She allowed as to how she really had to get the suitcase back or her brother would kill her, which could've been the truth. She watched me carefully as she elaborated that the suitcase contained all of her brother's latest software, which was about as far from the truth as you could get. I did my best to adopt the expression and the manner of an innocent bystander in New York. There are, of course, very few innocent bystanders in New York, and if they would please step forward I'm sure they would be T-boned by the Hampton Jitney.

For my part, I wailed a bit about the lack of security in the building, swearing up and down that this kind of thing had happened before and by God it really had to stop. I didn't, of course, mention the visit from the State Department boys or allude to the fact that the fraudulent passports were at that very moment sandwiched, in cat litter terms, several archaeological layers beneath the city of Troy.

Both of us gave rather convincing performances, I thought, and we vowed to meet again. Neither of us doubted that destiny would probably bring us together again. Because of circumstances beyond our control, neither of us was really looking forward to that occasion. In affairs of this nature, somebody always gets hurt.

"Of course the possibility always exists," I said to the cat, moments after Khadija's exit, "that the State Department *doesn't* have the suitcase. Khadija got into the loft this time. Maybe she or some of her gang got in before, took the suitcase, found the passports missing, and now they've sent her back to gain my confidence and find what I've done with the passports. She did give a pretty convincing performance, though."

The cat looked at me with pity in her eyes. Then she turned around abruptly and sat up stiff and straight with her back to me, her gaze firmly set on the far wall. As always, she had no trouble making her displeasure known.

"I wasn't referring to *that* performance," I said.

One power nap, one cigar, and one phone call from Rambam later, I'd left the cat in charge and was rattling uptown in a hack that appeared to be driven by the former president of Lesotho. I had a vague impression that he'd driven me before, but firm friendships are rarely forged in the big city. At least he drove more safely than the Pakistanis, more slowly than the Koreans, more accurately than the Haitians, and, apparently speaking no English at all, was far less inquisitive than the Israelis. If you judged a nation by the way they drove hacks in New York City, you could see why the world was in such a mess.

I got out of the taxi in sight of the Carlyle Hotel, and even though it was dark in the woods, it didn't take long for me to orb the highly incongruous cockroach van parked just down the street from the plush address. I'd stayed at the Carlyle myself before, sometime in the early ice age of the seventies. ABC-Dunghill Records had planted me there, provided the limo and the Peruvian marching powder, and proceeded to promote a record that all of us knew was going nowhere. Months earlier they'd fired Willie Nelson as my producer in Nashville and taken the project out to Hollywood with a handpicked producer from the record label. I knew I was in trouble the first day in L.A. as I looked through the glass in the studio and saw the guy applying clear polish to his fingernails.

About all I remembered about staying at the Carlyle was that during my brief time of residence Golda Meir was staying there, too. She'd been a kindergarten teacher in Milwaukee once. By the time she'd gotten to the Carlyle she was prime minister of Israel. Princess Diana, I reflected, as I moved through the darkness toward the surveillance van, had also once been a kindergarten teacher. There was something nice about people who'd once been kindergarten teachers, I thought. There was also something nice about Khadija, though I doubted if she'd ever taught kindergarten. If everyone was either a kindergarten teacher or a terrorist, it might not do much for the state of the world, I figured, but at least it'd make things easier for those of us scoring at home.

Of course, Golda wasn't staying at the Carlyle anymore. Now there was a decrepit van with a giant cockroach on top parked just down the street monitoring some golden retriever from the South of France in the process of seducing somebody I thought I cared about all for the purpose of McGovern freelancing a story about Rambam's ridiculous spy toys for some British tabloid.

I did not look forward with eagerness to hearing the sounds of Stephanie making love with some slick, as yet nameless asshole whom Stephanie would no doubt identify in the latter, more fever-ish phases of the lovemaking process. It was a hell of a way for a disgruntled suitor like myself to learn the guy's name. There was always the chance, of course, that Stephanie would resist his smooth advances. There was also the chance, I figured, that there'd be peace and freedom in the world. On the other hand, if you were ever going to hose somebody, the Carlyle Hotel was the place. And yet, as uncomfortable as I felt about the imminent sur-veillance of Stephanie, shadows of Khadija's fine features flitted through my mind to add to the already significant confusion. Did I love Stephanie, young ice princess, muse, dominatrix of my soul? Did I love Khadija, hot-blooded terrorist of my dreams whom Peace Corps guys like me always would be inclined to believe had a heart of gold? Would I ever fuck, suck, cajole, hose, or otherwise win the favor of either of these fair ladies without resorting to the phony, oily tissue of horseshit methods of some nameless asshole from the South of France? In Stephanie's case, things looked rather doubtful for the Kinkster. In Khadija's, however, I was pleased to admit that I had made some headway.

Summoning a cavalier spirit I did not truly feel, I knocked briskly on the side door of the van. The door slid open to reveal the small, dead face of a raccoon with its eyes sewn shut adorning the coonskin cap on top of Ratso's head. In proper international spy fashion he promptly put his finger to his lips and motioned me to follow him into the bowels of the van.

There were no headphones in evidence this time, but Rambam and McGovern both appeared to be hovering over a speakerlike device in the back of the vehicle. The van was silent as a tomb, the aura of anticipation almost palpable. Something exciting was about to happen in the city that had seen it all, heard it all, tried it all, died in the gutter and lived to tell about it.

"Perfect timing," said Rambam. "She's on her way up to the room."

27

I'D been in the market for a new laugh for about seven hundred years. The one I had sounded pretty much like an old wooden cross between the shriek of a wounded faggot and the maniacal keening of the Happy Wanderer. Fortunately, I rarely used my old laugh, so it never really attained the interpersonal irritation value it probably should've merited. But there was definitely something funny about the situation here. Rambam, Ratso, and McGovern seemed as serious as code-breakers in a World War II movie when in fact the only thing that was in any danger of breaking was my heart, and even that could probably be avoided if I could come up with a new laugh. There was, indeed, some humor in all this, but just as humor is a very close cousin to the truth, so it follows that it's harder to laugh when you begin to see that the joke is on yourself. And this goes beyond spying on the Stephanies of this world, if that notion could ever be pluralized, which I doubt. But I'm talking about the way life impersonally, implacably, yet giving the definite appearance of some kind of divine vendetta beats every single fucking one of us down whether we acknowledge it or not or just call it religion. Whether you're an English Channel swimmer who drowns in the bathtub, or a former prostitute who can't get laid, you'll probably get the cosmic joke sooner or later and you'll understand that whether God created man—as most kindergarten teachers believe—or man created God—as most college professors believe—both of them are pretty fucking perverse specimens. Man and God would make good alcoholic drinking buddies, kind of like Van Gogh and Gauguin except without the talent. You parents should tell your children that man is fucked, inescapably fucked. Tell them that God is a British gentleman walking around with white gloves and an umbrella and two thousand years of militaristic violence and other people's spilled blood in his veins and that he didn't write "Danny Boy." Tell them to get a new laugh every couple of years, trade it in on the old model, don't use it excessively in restaurants or public places because insightful individuals will recognize almost immediately that they are miserable.

"I put a spike mike in the door," Rambam was saying. "I would've preferred to have placed it in the wall of the adjoining room, but I'm afraid McGovern's meager budget precludes it."

"You're goddamn right," said McGovern. "I'm freelancing this fucking piece. Do you know what it'd cost to rent the adjoining suite in this hotel just to put a spike in the wall?"

"Maybe we should've put the spike in Ratso's forehead," I said. "Then the world could have constant encyclopedic knowledge of Hitler, Jesus, and Bob Dylan."

"Maybe we should've put the spike in *your* forehead," said Ratso. "Then we'd know what it's like to hose a terrorist. You *did* hose her, didn't you, Kinkstah?"

"Well—"

"You hosed a terrorist, Kinkster?" asked McGovern.

"Off the record," I said, "let's just say that I'm loath to engage in locker room talk and I'm proud to be an American—"

"Quiet!" said Rambam. "We're about to get something. It'll come through on all four speakers of the van. Sort of like Sense-Around-Stephanie."

"Fucking great," I said.

"That remains to be heard," said Rambam. "I still wish we could've set up and spiked the adjoining suite."

"What're you complaining about?" said McGovern. "I'm making you a fucking hero, Rambam."

"Famous last words," said Rambam, "of General Custer's executive butt-boy."

"Ah, bella!" said the four speakers in the van.

"Such a charming suite," said Stephanie, "for such a cute little count."

"He's a fucking count?" said Ratso.

"Shut up!" said Rambam.

"Champagne, bella?" said the voice of the man who was apparently a count.

"I'd love some," said the voice of the girl who apparently was about to succumb to the smooth advances of the man who was apparently a count.

"The spike mike beats the hell out of the pen mike," observed Ratso.

"Shut up!" said Rambam.

The silence inside the van was now deafening and the spike mike, indeed, was far superior to the pen mike. I never before realized how truly painful the small sounds of two people embracing can be. Ratso shrugged in embarrassment. Rambam had a sort of world-weary smirk on his face. McGovern smiled a brave smile that somehow never reached his Irish eyes. And the spike mike was ruthless. It got it all in quadraphonic sound.

"No one can beat a count, Kinkstah," said Ratso sympathetically.

"Shut the fuck UP!" said Rambam.

McGovern was now taking copious notes in his little notebook. What he was writing not to mention the entire scene itself was beyond my comprehension. How could Stephanie have fallen for this count? How could I have fallen for Stephanie? I wasn't sure if I was imagining slight rustlings of clothing or soft, guttural, dovelike cooing noises or if those were only the sounds of somebody's heart breaking.

"It's a small little thing, isn't it?" said Stephanie playfully.

"No one's ever told me that before," said the count.

"It's disappointingly tiny," said Stephanie.

"No one's ever brought it up," said the count.

"Maybe they couldn't see it," said Stephanie.

We continued to listen for some time but the spike mike had apparently gone to sleep. At last Rambam broke the silence.

"Christ, she's a cold bitch," he said.

"That's my girl," I said.

"I bet Count Baroque Dicko is having second thoughts about his courtship," said Ratso.

"Don't be so sure," said Rambam. "The spike mike doesn't lie. We'd know if she left the suite. They've probably gone into the bathroom or the bedroom and closed the door behind them, which would put the spike mike effectively out of range."

"It'd also put Stephanie effectively out of range for the Kinkster," I said rather grimly.

"Maybe they're doing something harmless, Kinkstah," said Ratso.

"Like what?" I said.

"They could be checking out the bidet," said Ratso. "They could be taking a bubble bath."

"Fucking great," I said.

"That remains to be heard," said Rambam.

As Allah willed it, we didn't hear any more that night. It became stultifyingly dull sitting in the van listening to our hair grow, so the subject quite naturally turned to my afternoon dalliance with Khadija. It was a coin toss, I figured, as to which engendered the larger share of social embarrassment: whatever was going on with Stephanie and the count, or whatever had not occurred between Khadija and myself.

"I know something happened with you two," said Ratso. "Rambam and I were monitoring the perimeter in case any of her gang showed up. You two were together alone for over two and a half hours."

"We talked," I said.

"And—" encouraged Rambam.

"And we searched for the missing suitcase."

"Your closet's about as big as my nose," said Rambam. "That must've taken all of thirty seconds. What else did you two do?"

"Yeah," said Ratso, getting ever more vicariously involved. "What's it like to hose a terrorist, Kinkstah?"

"Well, we didn't precisely hose—"

"Jesus Christ," ejaculated Rambam. "The way that broad was coming on to you, you could've hosed her with Ratso's penis."

"I wish he'd hosed her with my penis," said Ratso.

"What about McGovern's penis?" said McGovern, looking up briefly from his notes.

The whole drift of the conversation was making me vaguely uncomfortable. In the oral tradition of man, sexual intercourse is the ultimate achievement. Anything short of this awkward, ancient, largely overrated, often meaningless act usually raises other questions and other penises. Not only did I not wish to appear unmanly in the company of my friends, but I admit to feeling something else as well. Under the circumstances it was not entirely rational perhaps, but I felt oddly protective of Khadija's honor.

"I didn't hose her," I said.

"So all that time," said Rambam, "and you only got a blow job."

"Blow job's nothing to be ashamed of," said Ratso, though he did look a bit disappointed.

I said nothing further, which tended to confirm everybody's opinion that a blow job had indeed occurred. By this time it did seem almost anticlimactic.

Sometime later, under the assumption that there would probably be no further spike mike action, Rambam shut down the equipment and aimed the van toward the Village. Both Stephanie and Khadija had been forgotten and we were mainly oriented toward John's Pizza on Bleecker Street when out of the blue another country was heard from concerning the earlier discussion.

"A blow job given with love," said McGovern, as he gazed out the window of the van, "is as beautiful as dogs playing poker."

28

I come from a small, ill-tempered family. A happy childhood having left me hideously unprepared for life, I now whiled away the wintry nights sucking rather Freudianly upon a meerschaum pipe of JFK's head and reading occasional scraps of old newspaper articles to the cat. The cat had vomited into the JFK pipe some years previously and I'd given up pipe smoking for a while, but recently I'd carved out some of the crust with an old boning knife left behind by an Italian friend.

You never can quite get the essence of cat vomit out of a meerschaum pipe. It's just something you live with like a borrowed campfire or a blue train. The cat, no doubt, had forgotten the incident long ago, and as for myself, the words of Gandhi come to mind: Forgiveness is the ornament of the brave. And JFK like Christ Himself resting His bloodied head upon the grassy knoll that is the world, forgives all the cats who vomit in pipes, all the pathetic Lee Harvey Oswalds, all the tiresome conspiracy theorists and historical revisionists with the possible exception, of

126

course, of Oliver Stone, while the spirit of JFK lives on at the airport, in the Peace Corps, and, I'd like to think, next to the cat curled up in the rocking chair. I watched the rocker imperceptibly rocking as I sat at the desk with my JFK pipe, puffing secret Navajo signals to lesbians upstairs in the sweet and acrid smoke of life.

"Now here's a nice little obituary," I said to the cat, "sent to me by Kevin Carey's mother, Carolyn, in Denver. Kevin's a Peace Corps pal of mine who visited us at the ranch many years ago. You probably don't remember."

The cat, possibly mildly irritated by my failure to get right to the obit, did not seem to remember who *I* was. Undaunted, I continued my brief preface.

"Kevin's the last good lawyer in the world. He consistently turned down corporate offers in order to work with poor people, legal aid, immigrants, and the natives of Micronesia. Kevin did a lot of teaching on the island of Yap and came to know the Yappees pretty well. They honored him not as a lawyer but as a teacher, a profession they respected above all others. Obviously, a rather primitive culture. Kevin said that if you asked a Yappee what he thought about something, he'd stop, close his eyes, and concentrate deeply before answering. Imagine a group of people so backward that they actually stopped to think before they told you what they thought. Anyway, on to the obit."

The cat appeared to be slipping into a deep coma. If I intended to hold her attention at all I figured I'd better get to the meat of it. Cats are rather smug, perverse creatures and they often enjoy hearing details of the demise of other creatures not possessing nine lives.

"'Phillip McRae (Mac) Jones, 68, of Denver,'" I intoned, reading from the crumpled slip of newspaper, "'died February 23rd. Mr. Jones was born in Kilgore, Texas, June 18, 1932.

127

Cruelly denied by his youth an opportunity to vote for Herbert Hoover, he immediately withdrew into a petulant obscurity until he emerged from the University of Oklahoma in 1955 with a somewhat shaky degree in geology and a taste for oil exploration.'"

I glanced over at the rocking chair and noticed with some degree of gratification that the bright eyes of the cat were with me. On a cold, lonely night in New York with the threat of international terrorism hanging over your head, the eyes of a cat can sometimes guide your soul like two little lighthouses. I plodded on with the obit.

"'He married Susan Welty of Rockford, Illinois, on November 15, 1958, and he dragged her, loyal and uncomplaining, to garden spots like Midland, Los Angeles, and Houston, until they settled in Denver in 1980 to her everlasting relief. Susan preceded him in death on May 22, 1994, and he sorely missed her every hour since then until his own demise. . . . Mr. Jones and Sonny Wyman, the best partner a man could ever have, founded McRae and Henry in 1986 and actually survived in the oil and gas business much to their mutual surprise . . .'

"We're getting to the good part," I said, but I could see that no hype was necessary. A cat can sometimes tell you a worldful without saying a word.

"'Mr. Jones voted for Richard Nixon only once, and was uncommonly regretful afterward. A man can't have an experience like that and remain entirely cheerful for the rest of his life.'

"Killer bee," I commented, as the smoke of life gently drifted across the lively lyrics of death. "This guy's dead and he's more alive than many people I know. Most obituaries, you see, are written hastily by some grieving relative who probably never understood the stiff in the first place. They never get it right. This guy had the foresight to kick the ghostwriters to the curb and write the damn thing himself. He also demonstrates a sense of humor about life and death, which, whether you're alive or dead, is pretty fucking difficult to sustain. Reading this, as my father might say, makes you almost glad to be alive. Listen to the way he ends his own obituary.

"'The deceased requested that in lieu of flowers or the usual contributions to some damn fool charity, you spend the money on something giddy and silly and fun.'"

I looked at the cat and the cat looked at me and then, many stories above the lesbian dance class, Mac Jones ascended to heaven.

29

T H E cat, as I believe I've mentioned, had taken to dumping vindictively at various locations around the loft. This seemingly random, mean-spirited behavior actually had quite understandable psychological origins. The cat was motivated, of course, by a deep-seated sense of rejection caused by the fact that the litter box had now been in office almost as long the current pope. And the cat, it should be noted, was not alone in her studied avoidance of that lonely little litter box in the rain room. The agents from the State Department and the occasional terrorists passing through had eschewed it as well. Its only visitor these days, it seemed, was myself when I removed it temporarily from the tub in order to take a shower or when I plumbed its depths rather gingerly with the trusty boning knife to confirm that its contents remained intact and undisturbed.

"It's quite remarkable," I said to the cat, as I lit my first cigar of the morning, "how the most valuable, sought-after things in life can often be found in the last places anyone wants to look.

It's kind of like the Oscar Wilde story 'The Happy Prince.' You're familiar with it, aren't you?"

I knew, of course, that it was rather unlikely that the cat would be familiar with "The Happy Prince." All cats, however, have a fondness for, or at least a strong ambivalence toward, Oscar Wilde. They seem to revel in his boldness and sensitivity, yet at the same time they abhor the sense of scandal and social embarrassment that he brought upon himself. Be that as it may, you will never find a cat who won't listen to a story by Oscar Wilde.

"'The Happy Prince' is a wonderful children's story actually about a young prince who dies while masturbating as he was hanging himself from a shower rod and is reincarnated as sort of a living statue who can look over the city and see all the sorrows and tragedies of man. It is not really a children's story and, of course, the prince is not really very happy."

The cat's eyes fairly sparkled with curiosity. She was just perverse enough to be genuinely enjoying the story. This was a good thing because I hadn't heard from Stephanie, Khadija, or any other man, woman, or child in over twenty-four hours and my interpersonal relations were in danger of growing a bit rusty. If I could reach one person out there I figured I was a success.

"So the statue of the Happy Prince sees all this shit in the world and meanwhile he's covered with gold leaf and has eyes made of emeralds and it's getting cold as hell but he manages to befriend a little swallow who puts off his trip to Egypt in order to help the Happy Prince, who, of course, he realizes is totally miserable."

The cat said nothing but had now become clearly engrossed in the story. Whether her interest was sparked by Oscar Wilde's timeless tale, my not inconsiderable narrative powers, or the mention of the little swallow, God only knows.

"So the prince from high upon his pedestal sees all the

poverty and sickness in the city and keeps saying to the swallow: 'Swallow, swallow, little swallow, there is a child in a cold apartment without any food. Bring another gold leaf from my resplendent coat to her poor mother so that they can have something to eat.' And the swallow dutifully takes another fleck of gold from the statue and delivers it to its destination. It's getting really cold now and unless the swallow heads for Egypt very soon it will surely die but it doesn't want to leave the Happy Prince alone."

The cat, manifesting absolutely no sympathy for the plight or the flight of the little swallow, was now hanging on every word. The bond between the doomed bird and the denuded statue meant nothing to the cat. To hell with that shabby, misguided statue, she was probably thinking, I just want to eat that bird. It was not the first time, of course, that Oscar Wilde had been misunderstood.

"And the prince kept prevailing upon the bird. He'd say, 'Swallow, swallow, little swallow, there are two small boys living under a bridge . . . there's a starving playwright living in a freezing attic . . . there's an old widow with no wood for the fireplace . . . oh, swallow, swallow, little swallow, will you stay to help them just a little longer?'

"So the swallow stayed to help the Happy Prince help the poor, pathetic people of the city. When the glistening gold coat was all gone from the statue, at the prince's request, the little swallow with a breaking heart plucked out the emeralds from the statue's eyes to give to the needy.

"Winter finally came, of course. The little swallow froze to death, of course. Right at the foot of the fucking statue, of course. All the other birds had taken off for Egypt to frolic in the sun by the pyramids, but the little swallow stayed to help the Happy Prince help hopeless people, so it died at the foot of the Jesus of its choosin' who could no longer see without his emerald eyes and was starting to severely rust in the rain without his cloak of gold and when the little swallow died a strange metallic cracking noise was heard in the little square which scientists now believe to be the sound of a statue whose heart was breaking.

"So early the next morning the fucking mayor and the fucking town council, pardon my Shakespeare, were walking by the square and noticed how shabby the statue looked and they pulled it down and had it melted in a furnace. But the broken lead heart would not melt, so the workmen threw it on a dustheap where the dead swallow was also lying.

"'Bring me the two most precious things in the city,' said God to one of His Angels; and the Angel brought Him the leaden heart and the dead bird. 'You have rightly chosen,' said God, 'for in my garden of Paradise this little bird shall sing for evermore, and in my city of gold the Happy Prince shall praise me.'"

I got up from the desk and drew a hot espresso from the still gurgling machine, which loomed like a skyscraper over the little kitchen. I walked the espresso back to the desk, patted the cat on the head, and watched the late morning sunlight filtering feebly through the smoke and dust and gloom of the loft.

"It takes a brilliant and troubled homosexual poet," I said to the cat, "to write a story about a statue and a bird that is so beautiful it can reach across an ocean and a century just to touch a man and a cat."

The cat, of course, said nothing.

30

" P A C K A G E for Mr. Friedman," said the voice behind the door.

It was late in the morning now and I'd just awakened from a little power nap, and something about the way the guy was knocking sounded vaguely Middle Eastern.

"If this shit keeps up," I remarked to the cat, "it's going to put the puppet head out of business."

"Delivery for Mr. Friedman," came the voice again, relentless as a noxious vapor. It wasn't just the knock that sounded Middle Eastern I now realized; it was also the guy's accent. Of course, when you're predisposed toward terrorists invading your loft, you tend to imagine many strange things. Earlier that morning I could've sworn the espresso machine had been humming something from the *Scheherazade*.

By the time I'd become ambulatory and gotten to the door I'd cultivated a few second thoughts about opening it. Not for the first time I wished the door had one of those fish-eye peepholes that make everybody's face look like a carnival mirror so that even a small child selling Girl Scout cookies usually scares the shit out of you. On the other hand, it was almost Gary Cooper time and no terrorist in his right mind would launch an attack this early in the day. Besides, the guy's tone was that of a mild-mannered Middle Eastern type and thanks probably to some passing lesbian, the camel's nose was already in the tent.

I opened the door.

A young Middle Eastern–looking man, who as a kid probably threw rocks, was standing in my doorway looking mildly bored. He did not look like a terrorist except for his eyes, which were not kind like Jesus' or wise like Kahlil Gibran's. They were cold and clever and brown and they wanted something I didn't want to give them.

"A gift for you, Mr. Friedman," he said, handing me a small, cheaply wrapped package. "And now do you wish to give to me something you have that is ours?"

"If you're talking about the West Bank," I said, "this is hardly the time or place for a meaningful dialogue."

He smiled a brief, rueful smile that came about as close to his eyes as Moses ever got to reaching the Promised Land. It was not close enough to make me feel very comfortable.

"We will not come back if you give us what is ours," he said, turning away and heading down the stairs.

"What if I don't know what you're talking about?" I said, though both of us knew perfectly well what he was talking about.

"Then you will receive more gifts," he said ominously.

I stood in the cold hallway holding the package and listening for the young Arab's footsteps to walk out of my life. As they echoed dully down the stairwell, my eyes wandered for the first time in about two thousand years to the dusty little mezuzah that was nailed to the doorpost of my house. My mother had sent it to me years ago when I'd first moved into the loft, and Tom Baker, in a burst of misguided, drug-crazed, gentile fervor, had rushed to put it up on the doorpost, placing it unfortunately only a little bit higher than penis level. When this minor oversight was pointed out to him the next morning, Baker had graciously untacked the little silver scroll and placed it in the traditional position high up on the doorpost.

"What the hell were you thinking," I'd asked him at the time, "when you put that little booger up at scrotum level?"

"You never know," said the Bakerman, his Irish eyes twinkling, "when you're going to get a surprise visit from an Orthodox Jewish midget."

Now the Bakerman was gone and the mezuzah was still there, ostensibly blessing the house, but God knows what was inside the damn thing because nobody'd ever had the balls or the interest to crack one open. Nobody wanted six thousand years of bad luck. Supposedly, a tiny scroll was rolled up inside every one of the little dinguses, but only a few very religious Jews knew what was written on the little scroll, and it wouldn't've surprised me a hell of a lot if at the end of the Hebrew writing you discovered the words "No Deposit—No Return."

As I listened to the sound of the doors to the building close behind the young Arab messenger, I thought that it was always little things—little customs, traditions, objects, words—that meant virtually nothing if dissected on the lab table of modern science, yet that somehow determined and defined the difference between brotherly love and hatred amongst the peoples of the earth. How many harmless Don Quixotes and innocent Bedouin children and old ladies with three or more cats have died because of that dumb little cross around the neck of some fat girl in a laundromat in Buttflaps, Montana. I see you're wearing a six-pointed star. Why did your people kill our Lord? Just

136

something to do, I guess. As the Inca priest once said: "Pale men will come on floating houses." Poor Jesus never had a chance. There's no one to save Him from those He has saved.

I walked back into the loft, shut and locked the door behind me, placed the little package on the desk, and went over and warmed my hands in front of the fire. It felt suddenly very cold in the loft, not to mention the world. I walked back over to the desk and opened the little box. Inside the box was a mayonnaise jar filled with clear liquid. Floating in the liquid was a little finger. Around the finger was a little silver ring. It looked very similar to the one I'd recently seen worn by Khadija.

31

" W H A T the hell'd you expect from these people?" shouted Rambam over the blower sometime later. "A bar mitzvah present?"

Not knowing what else to do with it, I'd put the little jar and its macabre contents in the freezer for the time being. Now I was sitting at my desk listening to Rambam, puffing on a cigar, and pretending that every little thing was fine in the world and every little finger intact.

"These people play hardball even with their own," said Rambam. "It'll probably get worse before it gets better."

"What could be worse?"

"Don't ask," said Rambam.

He was right, of course. The finger in the jar was clearly a harbinger of things to come. Indeed, it almost seemed to be beckoning me forward to a place I dared not go.

"Look," said Rambam, "do you have a way of getting in touch with the other part of this Khadija person? I mean besides the finger?"

"Sure," I said. "I could page her at the fitness club or the nail parlor or maybe she's just picking up the kids—"

"You've got to find her."

"Well, she said she'd be calling me soon. But what does 'soon' mean to a terrorist?"

"It means any time before they kill you."

I puffed on the cigar and thought about it for a moment. There was no doubt that whoever had severed Khadija's finger would not hesitate to separate my head from my shoulders in order to get the passports. The only question was why hadn't they done it yet? The answer, I supposed, was that they had been through the loft thoroughly, hadn't found the passports, and realized if they croaked me they might never get them back. Whatever the next move was, I didn't want to be part of the game.

"Look," said Rambam, "they just got through giving you the finger—hey, that's pretty funny—they just got through giving you the finger—"

"That's a fucking knee-slapper—"

"Anyway, they're probably going to let you think about it for a while. I doubt if they'll come back today. I'll come by tonight and hold your hand if you want."

"It's too late to hold Khadija's hand."

"That's what you've got to establish. Is the finger in the jar really Khadija's finger? If it is, it means one thing. If it's not, it could indicate something entirely different."

"Like what?"

"I'd rather not go into it right now. Anyway, your job is to find this broad you met on the plane and see if she's missing a digit. Maybe you could casually check out the situation while she's giving you a hand job."

"That's funny as hell."

"Or maybe you could look her up in the Yellow Pages. Let your fingers do the walking."

"Let your asshole do the talking," I said.

After I'd cradled the blower with Rambam, things seemed ominously quiet in the loft. Where the hell was the lesbian dance class when you needed them, I thought? Moderately tedious as was his style, I had to admit that adhering to Rambam's advice was about the only way to go. You had to adhere to something or you might as well roll yourself in suppository form and fly off to the third ring of Saturn. I'd sit tight, I figured, until I heard from Khadija. But sitting tight, whatever you've heard about it, isn't always as easy as it sounds. There's also the danger if you sit tight long enough that you might risk the possibility of becoming a tight ass.

I'm not sure if it was God, Allah, or Hank Williams who was behind it all, but I was blessed with not having to loiter around the loft for the rest of my life. There were fates worse than loitering around the loft, of course, and one of them was currently residing in my freezer.

"Sometimes doing nothing's the hardest thing in the world," I said to the cat.

The cat, busily preening her whiskers, did not even cast a glare in my direction. She wasn't, of course, the only female who was currently ignoring me. Stephanie hadn't called. Khadija hadn't called. As the hours tediously ticked by I realized that all three of them had this trait in common: they came into your life just when you least expected them. In a sense, I reflected as I gazed out a rain-wept window into an empty street, all women were terrorists.

I'd completed my second Nixon and my third power nap, and I was just in the act of firing up my fourth cigar when the phones rang with almost a sentient urgency. I goose-stepped over to the desk and hoisted the blower on the left. All good little terrorists are usually on the left. All good little church-workers are usually

140

on the right. That's why all the rest of us are usually sandwiched in the middle of a worldful of horseshit and wild honey.

"Kinky!" sobbed the half-hysterical voice on the blower.

"Khadija?" I shouted, almost swallowing my cigar. "Is everything all right?"

"God, no!" she screamed. "Something horrible has happened!"

32

T H E only people who should ever be given the spiritual authority to ask the question "Is everything all right?" should either be a waitress or maybe a stewardess for Braniff Airlines. Everything is not all right, it never was, it never will be, and as I puffed a pacifying cigar and waited in the cold, drafty loft for the imminent arrival of a recently maimed, near-hysterical female terrorist, everything certainly wasn't all right now. I remembered something my father had once told my sister, Marcie, when she'd walked into the dark room in which he was sitting and asked, "Is everything all right, Father?" Tom had answered her in a way that was humorous, succinct, and cosmically truthful. "The last time everything was all right," he'd said, "was August 15th, 1945."

His eldest son was walking to the counter one generation later to pour a strong shot of Jameson's into the old bull's horn and everything was still not all right. I gave a brief, silent salutary toast to the puppet head on top of the fireplace, to the freezer compartment of the refrigerator and all it contained, and finally, to the past and all it contained, and I killed the shot. Everything was still pretty fucked up, but at least I was a swallow closer to Capistrano.

"Swallow, swallow, little swallow," I said to the cat. The cat looked at me with pity in her eyes.

I downed a quick second shot and realized the unconscious cosmic connotations of the words humorous, succinct, and truthful. They represented the initials of Harry S. Truman, the man who was one of the main architects of the reason Tom Friedman thought everything was all right on August 15, 1945. Humorous, succinct, and truthful were also elements of the current situation that found me waiting for the frozen fickle finger of fate to jab me in the left iris.

The humorous part of my predicament was that somebody'd given me the finger and I'd put it in the freezer. The succinct part was that if I didn't come up with a quick, decisive approach to the problem, Khadija's life as well as my own were in grave danger. The truthful part was that I felt something deeper than sympathy for Khadija. It was the wrong afternoon to sort through my emotions, however. When you're dealing with people ready and willing to inflict any manner of craven violence, it doesn't leave you a lot of time to discuss relationships. Even if you had all the time in the world, talking honestly and openly about your feelings with a woman who may be planning to blow New York City off the map is always somewhat problematic.

Watching from the window in the kitchen I saw her step hurriedly out of a taxi halfway up the block from the loft. Good terrorist tactics. The driver, if questioned later, would be vague about his party's destination. If the driver didn't speak English, he'd be even more vague. I watched Khadija move stealthily toward me. She was wearing a dark coat. She was also wearing gloves. It was a rather chilly evening.

It was painful for me to watch how clumsily she handled the puppet head. In my experience, of course, very few women have demonstrated any high degree of skill when it comes to catching a puppet head cleanly. This observation should not be taken to mean that they cannot excel in other areas of endeavor.

"My poor little terrorist," I said somewhat rhetorically to the cat. "What have they done to you?"

The cat watched the awkward puppet head retrieval from the windowsill with a rather jaundiced eye. She looked upon the world in the careless, arrogant manner of an aristocratic freak; yet, if the truth be known, she was a terrorist of sorts herself. I had seen embassies burn in her eyes.

I was back at my desk contemplating purchasing a chest hair wig and several medallions when Khadija walked in the door carrying the puppet head. She did not, I noticed, remove her gloves. I'd left the door unlocked for her, operating on the principle that when you know someone's a terrorist it makes it pretty hard for them to surprise you. Nevertheless, she did.

Almost before I could take in how stunningly beautiful were her desperate, tragedy-hewn, death-bound features, she was running like a dark, frightened child into my arms. I held her like a man who was drowning in teardrops and not all of them were hers. The little black puppet head, which she still gripped firmly in her gloved hand, smiled up at me reassuringly.

"I haven't held anyone this tight since the Tennessee Waltz," I said.

"You're the only one I can trust," she said. The words came low and soft on a fiber-optic line from the heart like a little girl talking to a teddy bear.

"Maybe it's time," I told her, "to come in from the cold."

Three stiff rounds of Jameson's later, I was sitting at my desk, Khadija was keeping the cobwebs off the client's chair, and the

144

puppet head was back on top of the mantelpiece smiling benignly upon the loft. The whiskey seemed to settle Khadija down a bit though not enough for the gloves to come off. I couldn't say that I blamed her.

"I shouldn't tell you this, but there's no one else I can talk to," she said. "They've kidnapped my brother."

"Who kidnapped your brother?"

"I don't know. There was blood leading to the hallway." She began weeping softly.

I wanted to help this girl as long as it didn't go so far as helping her blow up New York. I couldn't imagine turning her over to men in suits and ties and sunglasses, not as she was, all brotherless and fingerless and fragile as world peace. I did not delude myself that she was now an angel from the Koran. Once a terrorist always a terrorist, they say. But some former terrorists have become world leaders, even statesmen, even kindergarten teachers. I believed in second chances, but when you're dealing in the casino of life and death the stakes can be very high. I had a strong feeling, though, that an emotional sea change had occurred within Khadija. It was conceivable, of course, that I was just a sailor who'd been too long on spiritual shore leave.

"What'll I do?" said Khadija plaintively, as the cat jumped up upon the desk, possibly to comfort her, possibly to take advantage of the heat lamp.

"Well, we can't very well go to the police," I said. "We can't go to the State Department—"

"But you could help me," said Khadija. "You could help me find Ahkmed. He's a very dear brother."

"The one you said would kill you if you lost his—uh—software?"

Sand shifted in her eyes revealing a sorrowful biblical sister of my own heart. From deep in those earth-brown eyes I saw a future that would never be and a past that should never have been. It was a moment of truth that need not be spoken. We are all descended from the same Father. If there was a God, He was in Khadija's eyes.

"Who we are is not important," she said. "Or why we do the things we do. We are just two people thrown together in this crazy world who might possibly have the chance to save each other."

"Could be the beginning of a beautiful friendship," I said, breaking the connection with Khadija's eyes to watch the darkness descend upon Vandam Street.

"If not, it could be the end of everything," she said.

When I looked at her again she was stroking the cat but something was different. She'd taken off her gloves. At first I couldn't believe my eyes. Like a drunk taking a sobriety test, I struggled to rapidly count the digits on her hands. It couldn't be, I thought. But it was. Everything was intact. Both pinkies were there, including the one with the little silver ring.

I kissed her fingers and her eyes glistened slightly. If this was all an act, the girl deserved an Oscar nomination for Best Supporting Actress. The only question was, who was she supporting?

"I'm glad no one cut your finger off," I said.

"Who would do a thing like that?" said Khadija, still stroking the cat.

"That's what we're going to find out," I said.

33

A S my friend Captain Midnite says, I am a dreamer who never sleeps. That night, however, I slumbered as peacefully as a hibernating bear in the arms of my favorite terrorist. Khadija seemed to be sleeping peacefully, too, for there was just the beautiful hint of a little smile on her face. Maybe she was dreaming of finding a new life for herself with the Kinkster. Maybe she was dreaming of finding the passports and blowing up the building. I'd have given up my Sherlock Holmes head to know what she was dreaming, but I'd lost the 1-900 number for the dream police some years ago in California. I've never really cared much about what people think, but I do care about what they dream.

An act of rather explicit sexual nature did occur during the course of the night, and I include it here not for prurient titillation of any kind but for reasons which it is my hope will eventually become clear to even a puritanical descendant of the *Mayflower*. Without going into gratuitous detail, the act took place while most of me slept but one member of my body was wide awake. It was an act performed upon me by Khadija with such dexterity that it confirmed the presence of all of her fingers.

At dawn, while Khadija slept, I slipped furtively out of bed not even disturbing the cat. I got dressed quickly, grabbed a few cigars for the road, and headed out to an early morning prearranged dim sum meeting with Rambam on Mott Street in Chinatown. He'd pointedly asked me to come alone. I didn't feel really comfortable leaving the loft just then, but there was nothing I could do. When you've got a cat and a terrorist sleeping peacefully in your bed, it's a judgment call who you want to leave in charge.

The streets of the Village are beautiful early in the morning. They are innocent and almost hopeful, like an unsuspecting Nagasaki. The only times I remembered seeing the city this early was when I'd stayed up all night. On those occasions the city didn't look too damn good, mostly because I'd been snorting Peruvian marching powder all night and was hideously out where the buses don't run. It wouldn't take long, of course, for time to catch up with the city. I gave it about forty-five minutes.

I started to hail a hack on Hudson, but the chill morning air felt so good I legged it over to Canal, hooked a left, and kept going until I saw ducks hanging upside-down in the windows and I couldn't read the writing on the newspapers. Whatever was left of my rational mind told me I should not trust Khadija. But a still, small voice inside told me that there comes a time in anyone's life when you've got to trust someone whether you think you think you can trust them or not, or else the part of you that you always wanted to be when you grew up may cease to exist entirely and you'll never again be able to trust yourself. Or something like that, I thought, as I walked into the dim sum place, ankled it up a flight of stairs, and sat down at a large round table that was currently occupied by Rambam and an entire extended Chinese family.

"Welcome to *Seven Brides for Seven Brothers*," said Rambam, as he sucked a large black snail. "Did you bring the finger? It might go well with the chicken feet."

"I brought this finger," I said, flipping him the bird to the amusement of one little Chinese kid who'd been staring at my cowboy hat. The rest of the extended family was not amused.

"What took you so long getting here?" said Rambam.

"I walked from the loft," I said. "I just wanted to think. By the way, it's not her finger."

"If that finger's not hers, then you'd better think fast," he said.

"As the psychologist said, 'What do you mean by that?'"

"I mean I don't think Khadija's guys sent you the finger. If they'd bothered to send anything, they'd've sent you the real fucking thing. It's too subtle a ploy for your fundamental fundamentalist, if you get my drift. Finesse is not the calling card of Arab terrorists."

I looked at Rambam, mystified. The Chinese family looked at Rambam, mystified. They obviously spoke almost no English but every once in a while they'd give a little tentative smile in our direction, as if they understood a word or two. Rambam or I would give them an almost half-conscious tentative smile in return. It amounted to some of the most satisfying communication I'd had with anybody in years.

"So you're saying that—"

"Somebody else has come to the party," said Rambam.

The party was already unpleasant enough, I thought, as I chopsticked a shrimp ball the size of a golf ball into my mouth.

"They're sure catching large shrimp these days," said Rambam.

"So who sent the finger?" I said, after chewing the shrimp ball ninety-seven times. "The State Department?"

"Not their style. They've probably been keeping an eye on

149

you, though. Have you seen any black helicopters circling around above the lesbian dance class?"

"I've noticed a black helicopter circling around your brain," I said. "So if it's not the State Department, who is it? The FBI?"

"Are you kiddin'? They're still busy trying to blow up Castro's fucking cigar. They don't know he quit smoking."

"What about the CIA?"

"They're busy destabilizing half the governments of the world. Speaking of destabilizing, where do you think this Khadija broad is now?"

"I think she's back in the loft in my bed. We spent the night together."

"Isn't that fucking romantic? You've got to be a fucking god-damn idiot!"

The Chinese grandmother smiled tentatively at Rambam. He was trying to control his chopsticks, so I smiled tentatively back.

"So who the hell sent me the phony finger?"

"For my money?"

"Your money's no good here."

"I can't prove it yet, but I believe it could be the same guys who invented matzo."

I smiled tentatively at Rambam. He responded with a rather wicked smirk.

"That's right, pal," he said. "The Israelis."

R A M B A M and I got back to the loft a little before nine, just about the time most busy top executives were straightening their ties and preparing to plunge into the spirit-grinding work-day ahead. Rambam and I, of course, had work to do, too. We simply weren't quite sure what it was. When you're dealing with terrorists, sometimes you've just got to wait for the other bomb to drop. In our particular case, we didn't have to wait very long.

I kicked on the espresso machine at Rambam's repeated insistence, then tiptoed into the bedroom to check on Khadija. The cat was the only one on the bed. She was lying comfortably with her head on the pillow and she seemed moderately irritated by my untimely intrusion.

My mind lit up like a Christmas tree in Las Vegas, overloading all the circuits with hopes and doubts and fears and scenarios. Had Khadija been abducted from the loft? Was the story about her brother's kidnapping merely another way to gain my sympathy and confidence? Had she simply gone home, if, indeed, she had one? Was she going it alone, desperate and distraught, amongst the uncaring people on the mean streets of a foreign city? I never really thought that the two of us would live happily ever after. No one ever does. It was something you couldn't quite put even somebody else's finger on, but it troubled me immensely. A rare opportunity of some unique kind had been lost, I felt. It was irrational, of course, and it might've been as simple as a girl leaving a guy, but there seemed something inescapably sad about Khadija's abrupt departure from the loft that morning.

It was a grief all out of proportion to the situation, I realized, as I walked out into the living room. Of course there were things we could've done together. Of course there were things I should've told her. Instead, I put it all into two words to Rambam, who was loitering around in the hallway outside the rain room.

"She's gone," I told him.

"You think that's bad," said Rambam, "you ought to see what's in the dumper."

34

TECHNICALLY, I suppose, the man was not *in* the dumper. He was very definitely, however, *on* the dumper. Rambam, of course, had used the word "dumper" to describe the entire confines of the rain room. I, however, had understood his statement in its narrowest interpretation to mean in the dump machine itself. I thought he was making some form of crude joke at first, but I was quickly disabused of that notion. The man was sitting on the dumper all right, but he was fully dressed and the lid was down. His lid was down, too, apparently. Somebody'd put a bullet through it.

"This is *exactly* what I didn't want to happen," I said, quoting my father.

I walked closer to the body. The guy had definitely been relegated to the past tense department. He looked like a statue of *The Thinker.*

"We'll have to call the cops," said Rambam. "If for no other reason, sooner or later one of us is going to have to take a dump."

"I'm not going to take a Nixon in there for at least twenty-seven years," I said.

"Is that healthy?" said Rambam.

If you find the rather puerile nature of this conversation somewhat surprising, you've probably never stumbled upon a dead body. It's a fact of human nature, whether the stumblee is an amateur or a hardened professional, that graveyard humor of some sort is invariably employed in the initial discourse. Psychologists tell us that this form of morbid humor is a defense mechanism to protect the unprepared human psyche from the shock of momentarily teetering on the brink of mortality by witnessing the stark reality of death. They do not tell us if it is particularly humorous to stumble across the body of a dead psychologist.

The dead man on the toilet looked to be of Arab descent, but the blood on his clothes—on the porcelain, on the bathroom floor—was as red and as real as any red-blooded American's. He was young-looking, and he was dressed, according to Rambam, in the latest trendy terrorist sartorial style—tennis shoes, jeans, black T-shirt, black nylon zip-up windbreaker. The expression on his face, beyond a shadow of a doubt, was as if he'd just received the surprise of his life.

"Jesus Christ," said Rambam. "Do you see what he's holding in his right hand?"

"Yeah," I said, moving farther into the rain room, "it looks like a pager or beeper or walkie-talkie of some kind."

"That really fucking bothers me."

"You've got a dead man in the dumper and the fact that he's holding a walkie-talkie is what's worrying you? I don't care if he's holding a *Wall Street Gerbil*. He's been croaked right here in my loft. That's what bothers me."

"But doesn't this suggest something to you, Inspector Maigret?"

"It suggests that we should call the cops right now," I said as I started to scurry out of the dumper.

"Not so fast," said Rambam, grabbing my arm. "This stiff isn't going anywhere. I'm not going to touch anything, but I do want to have a closer look at the crime scene. Any good little private investigator would want to check a few things for himself, and you should, too."

I knew Rambam was right, but it was a very uncomfortable, restless feeling to be in that small room with a guy who'd been so recently croaked. No one has ever accused the Kinkster of being squeamish. It wasn't that. It was more like a heady sense of déjà vu that I was experiencing. The man currently occupying the throne was not the first guy to get himself croaked in this rain room. Years ago the Gypsy in the bathroom mirror had witnessed an even gorier murder in which a shotgun had totally removed the face of the unfortunate victim. This current croakee appeared to be the victim of a far more professional killer. The circumstances had been entirely different, of course, but through a careful chain of deductive reasoning I was beginning to conclude that this was a bad-luck dumper.

"At least the cat litter tray appears to be intact," I said, as I pulled back the shower curtain and peered into the tub.

"Which is more than you can say for this guy's head."

"All that blood and damage from just one bullet?"

"Yes, Miss Marple, that's the way it looks."

"You don't think Khadija could've killed him?" The thought hit my brain with the intensity of—for the want of a better metaphor—a speeding bullet.

"Yes, Miss Marple, that's the way it looks."

"But what was this guy doing here on the dumper in the first place?"

"That's one the cops'll have to answer," said Rambam,

crouching down to study the walkie-talkie in the dead man's hand.

"That's good," I said, "because I'm calling them right now."

I goose-stepped out of the rain room, but, unfortunately, I did not get a chance to call the cops. In this short and troubled dream we sometimes think of as life, a hell of a lot can happen between the dumper and the blower.

35

" **H E Y !** " shouted Rambam from the dumper. "This isn't a fucking walkie-talkie!"

I started to ask "What is it?" but I never got past the word "What." A viselike arm encircled my neck and I felt the round, hard, phalliclike impression of a gun squarely in the small of my back. Before I could think of reacting to this rather unpleasant situation, another man, dressed almost identically to the stiff on the dumper and carrying a gun himself, came catapulting through the now mysteriously open kitchen window. Out of the corner of my left eye I observed two more identically dressed dark forms move in an almost dreamlike fashion from the front door into the dumper, guns drawn. They were men of few words and those they did speak were uttered in gruff, guttural, Middle Eastern accents. The phrase I remember in particular was spoken by the guy with the gun in my back. I still couldn't see the guy, but I recall rather vividly the question he posed: "Do I kill this cowboy here?"

Apparently that wasn't the immediate plan, for the next thing I knew, the four of them were hustling Rambam and myself out of the loft at gunpoint. The cat sat on the kitchen counter and watched the whole ugly scene play out with an expression of mild irritation on her face. This is the basic difference between a dog and a cat. A dog would've at least bitten somebody on the ass for whatever it would've been worth, or surely barked loudly enough to wake up a dead lesbian. The cat, on the other paw, merely scratched what I suspected was an imaginary flea and continued to watch us being violently hustled out of the loft, with nothing more than a look of slightly peeved indifference crossing her unruffled countenance. There is, of course, a great lesson in life here for all of us: if you even vaguely suspect that you might be abducted by ruthless Islamic terrorists, always remember to feed the cat her tuna before you go out to meet Rambam for dim sum in Chinatown. If all the peoples of the world could learn this simple lesson, the earth would be filled with far happier people, far more contented cats, and far fewer terrorists. In our particular case, unfortunately, this lesson was learned just a bit too late.

It was a little after nine A.M. when our party hit the hallway. I didn't know if these guys had been doing reconnaissance or not, but they certainly seemed to know the lay of the loft and the building. They also appeared to be surprisingly well organized. Almost like it had been carefully planned, two of them escorted Rambam into the little elevator while the other two hustled me down the stairs. I had four floors' worth to think things over and I didn't much like where my thoughts or these characters were taking me.

Somebody'd once asked Rambam if I were a practicing Jew. He'd told them: "If he is, he needs to practice a little more." That having been said, however, when you're being taken at gunpoint from your loft and your cat by desperate, swarthy, sullen,

Islamic fundamentalists, the fact that you're Jewish does tend to linger in your mind for about forty years in the desert.

It was ironic, I reflected, as we rounded the third-floor stairwell, how very crowded New York City always is except when you really needed it to be. Usually you could count on running into some ambulatory form of humanity in the hallways of 199B Vandam at this hour of the morning. At the moment, I'd have been happy to bump into a lesbian, a rambling hunchback, a door-to-door methadone salesman, a lost outpatient with a Bowie knife, or a determined teenager on his way to commit an act of autoerotic asphyxiation. I wouldn't have even minded coming face-to-face with Stephanie's count on his way upstairs for eggs-bend-my-dick. But, of course, this morning there was nobody. The hall was as empty of humanity as an ex-lover's eyes.

"Do you get to New York often?" I said as we reached the second-floor landing, striving to break the stifling silence.

"Shut up," said the guy behind me, jabbing the gun viciously into my back again.

That killed the conversation until we reached the little lobby and stood around for a moment like three guys waiting for an elevator. I always knew it was a slow elevator, but I'd never scientifically timed it before with two groups of terrorists acting in tandem. From the look of things, I would not live long enough to compare my data with other pointy-headed intellectuals. My two abductors seemed grim, ruthless, highly motivated, and very professional, and they didn't appear nervous about flashing their guns around in broad daylight, something that might've given your everyday garden-variety mugger a moment's pause. At least they weren't firing their weapons and shouting "Allah Akbar!" That, very possibly, came later. If there was a later.

As the machinery in my mind raced in a million different directions, the elevator made a loud clanking noise and the doors opened very briefly. Rambam leapt out like a kangaroo, the doors closed behind him, and his two escorts found themselves on a mandatory trip to the basement. Meanwhile, the tiny lobby had suddenly turned into a zoo and a half with Rambam and one of the terrorists struggling for a gun while the other gunman futilely tried to cover both of us with his weapon.

"Open the fuckin' door!" Rambam shouted to me, as he kneed his dancing partner in the balls and cartwheeled him into the second terrorist.

It was strange that not a shot had been fired, but I didn't give a lot of thought to that fact at the time. I was so busy running for my life that I almost got T-boned by a moving garbage truck and went sprawling into the street. By the time I got to my feet, the truck was moving slowly past me and I jumped onto the side as it rolled by and hung on for dear life. Before I could blink, Rambam had leapt onto the truck beside me and from somewhere on his body had pulled a weapon of his own.

"Didn't you always want to be a garbageman when you were growing up?" said Rambam.

"No," I said. "I wanted to be a black Baptist preacher."

"Never hurts to aim high," said Rambam, just as one of the terrorists, gun in hand, jogged into sight behind the truck.

Then the garbage truck stopped.

The terrorist drew a bead on Rambam and Rambam drew a bead on the terrorist. Like an old western movie the tension mounted as I entertained rather fanciful visions of rolling past the pearly gates on the side of a garbage truck. Just as St. Peter was offering me a line of Peruvian marching powder from a shining silver mirror in the sky, the garbage truck jolted into motion again. As we rounded the corner, the terrorist, apparently having had enough, disappeared down Vandam Street.

"It's a good thing we didn't run into some officious, conscientious garbageman," I said, "who might've stopped the truck and made us get off."

"Never happen in New York," said Rambam, with something close to pride in his voice. "There's no such thing here as a conscientious city worker. You could have the entire Gay Men's Choir of Manhattan riding on the side of this garbage truck, and they wouldn't give a shit."

"How about a song?" I said.

36

I called the cop shop from a pay phone in front of a health food bar on Hudson Street. I wasn't sure how healthy I was, but after what Rambam and I had just been through, it did feel almost good to be alive. After several underlings passed the baton back and forth a bit, I finally got through to Detective Sergeant Mort Cooperman. He was never happy to hear from me and he was even less so after I told him what was waiting for him at 199B Vandam Street.

"Let's see if I have this right, Tex," said Cooperman irritably. "You just waltz into your loft this morning and at a little before nine you find a stiff on your dumper?"

"That's correct, Sergeant."

"And why did you wait so long to call us?"

"Islamic terrorists abducted me from my loft, but I managed to elude them by hitching a ride on a garbage truck."

"That's very fucking funny, Tex. But I do take it you're serious about the stiff on the throne?"

"That's correct, Sergeant."

"Okay. One question though, Tex. Just routine, you under-stand. This dead guy on the dumper. Was he a fat guy in a fancy suit?"

"I'm afraid not."

"Okay, so it ain't Elvis. It was just a thought. Got to cover all the bases. We'll check it out, Tex."

The last thing I heard before Cooperman cradled the blower was a loud, grating chortle that came down the line like a guy starting up a leaf-blower at Walden Pond. It was probably a good thing, I reflected, that Cooperman didn't appear to buy my story about the terrorists. Now, if he and his boys would just forklift the corpse out of the rain room without finding the passports in the litter box or the finger in the freezer, everything would be back to about as normal as it ever gets.

"Get through to Cooperman?" asked Rambam, as he joined me for the slow walk back to the loft, a place I wasn't going to go back into until I saw it surrounded in plain-wrapped squad cars.

"Yeah, I talked to him," I said. "He wanted to know if the dead guy on the dumper was Elvis."

"That's pretty funny. I didn't know Cooperman had a sense of humor."

"He doesn't. Look, there's one thing that's bothering me. When that terrorist aimed at us to pick us off the side of the garbage truck, what stopped you from just shooting the bas-tard?"

"I couldn't be sure he was an Arab."

I thought about it for a moment. It might've made sense in Rambam's mind, but the logic managed to elude me even more swiftly than we'd eluded the terrorists. If it looks like a terrorist, walks like a terrorist, and pulls a gun like a terrorist, for my money it's probably a terrorist.

"You're telling me," I said, "that because the finger wasn't Khadija's, you think these guys might've been Israelis trying to infiltrate the terrorist cell? That little finger's pretty slim evidence."

"The phony finger was only the first clue," said Rambam, warming to the subject. "The fact that they could've shot us and didn't is another. It's kind of like spy versus spy. You can't tell Arabs from Israelis and that's the way they like it."

"I'm glad *they* like it," I said, "because *I* don't."

"If we ever figure out who they are, I'll tell them. But I haven't gotten to the main reason I think these guys are Israelis. It's the walkie-talkie in the dead man's hand. I don't think it's a walkie-talkie."

"What do you think it is? A garage door opener?"

"No, asshole. I think it may be a receiver. I also think there may be a transmitter somewhere among the passports."

"I didn't see one."

"Of course not. Neither you nor I were looking for one, and you wouldn't have known what to look for anyway. A fucking transmitter can be the size of a credit card. It could've easily been sewn into the back of one of the passports."

"So the dead guy on the dumper followed the signal to the loft and all the way into the rain room, then couldn't find the passports and so he sat down to think it over."

"That's the way I see it. Once the cops clear out we can check the passports for the transmitter. If it's there, it proves the guy on the dumper, and probably the four supposed terrorists, weren't really terrorists at all."

"How does the transmitter prove that the dead guy wasn't a terrorist?"

"Because the Arabs have no reason to put a transmitter in the passports. It's their deal. They just drop them off and pick them

163

up, and that's what would've probably happened if you hadn't been such a good little citizen and taken that pink suitcase home with you from the airport. What we don't know is whether the guys who planted the transmitter—assuming there is one—are from the State Department or the State of Israel. They could also be CIA, FBI, or possibly agents of the counterrevolutionary count that Stephanie hosed at the Carlyle."

"We don't know that Stephanie hosed the count at the Carlyle."

"Just employing a little deductive reasoning, Sherlock. By the way, do we even know for sure that the passports are still there? I know the litter box looked intact, but maybe Khadija took them with her and carefully covered her tracks, as it were."

"All I know is that the three dried cat turds that have been carbon-dated back to the Shroud of Turin all seemed to be in the same position."

"Which is pretty much the same position we're in except we don't know shit. All I know is that the dead guy ain't Elvis and we could've both gotten killed this morning. In the future don't be such an obliging dupe. Next time you meet a broad on a plane, tell her to go fuck herself."

"Now you tell me."

We were well in sight of the loft now. Several squad cars were parked on the sidewalk amidst a flotilla of garbage trucks. Uniforms and techs were coming and going from the building. I had to admit I felt more secure than I'd felt all morning. Rambam clapped me heavily on the shoulder as a form of encouragement. Then he headed back up Vandam away from the loft.

"Why don't you come up with me?" I suggested.

"Cops make me sneeze," said Rambam.

37

M O M E N T S later, I was being rather unceremoniously hustled up the same four flights of stairs that the terrorists had so recently rather unceremoniously hustled me down. The purloined passports, I reflected, as a large uniform puffed along beside me, had truly become the bottle imp of my life. The appearance of the terrorists, or infiltrating spies as Rambam believed, indicated that something very big was being plotted here. The stakes had been raised way over someone like Cooperman's head and it was getting a little dicey even for someone like myself to remain in this deadly and dangerous game. I knew Cooperman would probably never find the passports, but just in case his boys stumbled across the frozen finger, Rambam had suggested telling them it was a small, oddly shaped piece of herring. I doubted if even the NYPD would be that slow out of the chute, however—you don't often see a small, oddly shaped piece of herring wearing a little silver ring.

One thing was for sure. As long as I held the passports and almost everybody suspected that I had them, my life was going to read like the tawdry pages of a cold war spy novel populated by Arabs, Israelis, State Department types, CIA, FBI, fingers in mayonnaise jars, and corpses on commodes. Compared to all this foreign intrigue, dealing with the cops ought to be a piece of cheesecake at the Carnegie Deli. Yet Cooperman's first words as I entered the loft filled me with dread and trepidation.

"Hey, Tex!"he shouted. "I think it's about time you changed that cat litter box."

"Seven years isn't up yet," I said, as casually as I dared.

"Reason I mention it," continued Cooperman, "is the cat just took a dump on your desk."

The cat shit gods must've been smiling on me, I figured, as I ventured a glance into the rain room, then walked over to the desk and verified Cooperman's observation. You couldn't even see the corpse in the rain room because of the large assistant medical examiner and the handful of techs studying the crime scene. But you could see, just by looking at the desk, that a small mammal had passed that way recently.

"This guy on the shitter, Tex," said Cooperman. "He a close personal friend of yours?"

"Never seen him in my life," I said, as I scooped a rather large specimen of cat manure onto the front page of *The New York Times*.

"Any idea who whacked him?" asked Cooperman.

"Not even the vaguest," I said, which wasn't terribly far from the truth.

"The victim has no identification, but he's left his prints all over the place. You go about your business for a while. We're going to be dusting the place."

"Good," I said. "The place needs dusting."

"Very funny, Tex. But just so you know. We don't do windows and we don't pick up cat turds. Now get out of my sight."

166

I used the respite from Cooperman to locate the cat (she was under the davenport), bring her back to the desk with me, light up my JFK pipe, and wonder why the hell I was so tenaciously hanging on to the damn passports in the first place. I could've just given them back to Khadija. Or given them to the State Department. Or the Israelis, if they really were Israelis. If the guy on the pot and the four "terrorists" were Mossad agents, why wouldn't they just tell a fellow hebe like myself? Why try to abduct Rambam and myself? On the other hand, if they were really Arab terrorists, why didn't they blow us away? The guy on the dumper had gotten awful close to pay dirt before somebody'd blown him away. That was the guy to constipate on. Was he an Arab or a Jew? If the cops ever cleared out, we could check the passports for a hidden transmitter. If we found one it would prove he'd been one of the good guys. This, of course, is not to say that all Jews are good and all Arabs are bad. In fact, the only discernible difference between the two cultures that I've been able to observe is that, while both groups traditionally eschew pork, of the two, the Jews more aggressively pursue pork belly futures.

On a sperm-of-the-moment impulse, I called my favorite Arab in the world, Jimmie "Ratso" Silman, in my nation's capital. Washington Ratso, as I sometimes called him to distinguish him from the far more repellent New York Ratso, was a Lebanese Druse guitar player and TV news reporter who'd been my friend for over twenty-five years. He had twenty guitars, eighteen large king snakes, one mustache that looked like Saddam Hussein's, and one sign over his dumper that read COLORED MEN.

"Greetings, my Bedouin brother," I said, when Ratso picked up the blower.

"Ah, how's it hangin', heebie-jeebie of my heart?"

"That's what I wanted to talk to you about. Ratso, are you circumcised?"

"Things've been a little slow around here lately," said Ratso. "I'm not sure."

"Check for me," I said patiently, watching a tech dust the espresso machine for prints. "It's important."

"Well, what do you know?" said Ratso jubilantly. "I *am* circumcised!"

"Are most Arabs circumcised, though? I mean, does Islam teach circumcision?"

"Of course it does. Don't you think we want to be just like you guys when we grow up? Why are you whispering?"

"Because there are more cops in the loft right now than you've got king snakes. There was a guy iced on my dumper this morning and I don't know if he's an Israeli spy or an Arab terrorist."

"Is he wearing a lot of gold chains?"

"No, Ratso. No identifying features of any kind. He's just a Middle Eastern type with a mustache like yours and Saddam Hussein's."

"Then he's probably an Arab."

"Then why would he want to bug a batch of fraudulent passports? Why would he follow the signal all the way into my rain room? Why would he die with a receiver in his hand? Why didn't four supposed Islamic terrorists dressed just like him shoot me and Rambam this morning?"

"What the hell is this?" said Ratso. "The Four Questions?"

For a Lebanese Druse Christian, Ratso was better versed in Jewish culture and religion than many Jews. He'd grown up with Jews, most of his friends were Jews, and I wasn't entirely sure, but I thought I was beginning to detect a faint rather irritating whine in his vocal intonations.

"Look," said Ratso, "you basically can't tell a dead Jew from a dead Arab. That doesn't mean there aren't subtle traditional differences between them when they're alive. The way they pray, the way they enter a house, the way they eat a meal, the way they're married, the way they're buried, the way they take a dump—"

"That'll be fine, Ratso. Actually, you've been a big help."

"No problem," said Ratso. "Now how about the West Bank?"

I relit JFK, patted the cat on the head, and bugged out for the hallway where Detective Sergeant Buddy Fox was smoking a cigarette and studying the occasional passing lesbian. Ratso had given me an idea. It was crazy, but it might just fly. Fox was in what was for him a fairly engaging mood.

"Next time you got a problem with the toilet, call the fucking plumber," he said.

"I'll remember that, Sergeant. By the way, as long as your guys are dusting everything in the loft besides the cat and myself, how about having them knock out this little booger while they're at it?"

I gestured offhandedly with JFK to the dusty little mezuzah on the door frame. Fox allowed his jaundiced eyes to crawl slowly up the doorpost like a pair of garden slugs. After they reached the tiny religious object in question, they shifted and studied me briefly. At last, Fox made an executive decision.

"What the hell do I care?" he said. "We get paid by the hour."

He waved a tech over and soon the guy was busily at work dusting the mezuzah. Fox and I stood in the hallway and supervised.

"No favor too small or meaningless if it's for a friend," Fox said, glaring at me sullenly. "But that's a cop's lot in life. I got a corpse on the crapper and here we are dusting this little bastard. What do you call that thing anyway? A mazola?"

"I always had you lamped for a closet Jew, Fox."

"Forget the closet," he said, "and forget the Jew."

"I've tried both," I said, "but nothing works."

38

AFTER the cops cleared out the corpse and cleared out themselves, I cleaned up the loft a bit and then cleared out a space on the couch to crash with the cat. Outside the window it was cold and dark and getting colder and darker. Inside the loft the merry fire in the fireplace was doing its damnedest to drive off the spooky vibratory area that always exists for those of us who insist upon concealing much coveted contraband in the cat litter box. So far, hiding the passports had only brought me grief and if I held on to them much longer it was certainly possible that I might not be able to continue to navigate the cold, choppy waters that spilled the lifeblood of saints and pen pals into the river of darkness that constituted the difference between the merely being and the human being.

"I've got to get rid of these fucking passports," I said to the cat.

The cat, of course, said nothing, but there was a decidedly wistful expression in her traffic light eyes as they changed like a silent season from green to yellow. Perhaps she remembered Khadija's kindnesses to her. Perhaps she believed the proper thing to do was wait patiently for Khadija's return and then go hand in hand with the passports to the State Department where agents with the borrowed names of former presidents would smile upon us benignly and thank us for our public service and send us out into the world to live happily ever after. It was a great hope, but it was not to be. A cat knows little of the world of man unless it wanders into a dark alley someday and meets a group of small boys who tie a string of tin cans to its tail.

"Maybe I'll give the passports to that guy in India who drinks his own urine," I said.

To this suggestion the cat responded with a mild moue of distaste. This was wildly ironic in that the cat had had no qualms whatsoever in taking a recent Nixon under the rocking chair.

I was beginning to run out of small talk when I heard the rain-like, xylophonelike sounds from the fire escape outside. Pale men will come on floating houses, I thought. Olive-complected men with mustaches will creep up stairs of iron. They'd already gotten as far as the rain room. Now they were coming again. Coming for my precious passports.

In the direction of the dumper through a Dead Sea of wet cement, I ran with all my might. Into the rain room and out again carrying the cat litter tray, heading for the hallway. I had to preserve the passports for Khadija's sake. God, Allah, or L. Ron Hubbard had sent this Arab beauty to me to show that love's not only blind, it also has attention deficit disorder.

Up the stairs I ran with a legion of olive-complected men closing in behind me. I crashed through the door of Winnie Katz's loft where a number of her girls were working on a rather zippy retro swing number. Through Winnie's loft I ran, carrying the cat litter box like a pizza tray, disrupting the class, causing Winnie

171

to become highly agitato, unable to explain because I had a cigar in my mouth and was carrying a pizza tray and running for my life from men who were carrying wildly beeping receivers which made them Israeli spies and men who were wildly firing weapons which made them Arab terrorists and the whole macho parade failing to arouse or interest the girls in the slightest, which, of course, made them lesbians.

Out Winnie's window and down the fire escape I ran, still clutching the cat litter tray and continuing to waste my entire adult life vainly pursuing the Vulva of the South. Down Vandam Street I flew through the night swifter than childhood, the cat litter and the occasional cat turd streaming over my shoulders into the feverish, fulvous eyes of my pursuers, and yet they came. One terrorist in particular had closed the distance quite a bit and now was running right behind me. He'd been in trouble with the law before, or so I was told later, but apparently had gotten a charge of sodomy reduced to following too closely.

At last, as more shots rang out, I threw the litter tray into the night and hopped aboard a double-parked magic carpet. Khadija piloted us straight through till morning and we ran into a St. Peter type who offered me another line and said: "Welcome to Clever-Clever Land. May I please see your passport?" Khadija, of course, shot me a dirty look. "In the words of the great Levon Helm," I told the guy, "'We have nothing to declare. All we had is gone.'" He waved us right through to God's waiting room where we spent the lifetime of John Keats or Gram Parsons (God told us later that they were actually the same person) listening to a Muzak version of the Beach Boys' "Good Vibrations." I was gratified to note that the Muzak version retained the cello part that had been written and performed by Van Dyke Parks on the original recording. I had just started to peruse "The Giant Rat of Sumatra" by Arthur Conan Doyle when God's receptionist, who bore an uncanny resemblance to Princess Di, came in and said, "Let's step lively, folks. God's got a golf engagement with Allen Ginsberg, Frank Sinatra, and Townes Van Zandt, and after that he's got a luncheon date with Mama Cass."

"God plays golf?" I asked.

"Miniature golf," she said.

Every small child has a pretty clear picture of God which he keeps in his heart. God either looks like Hoss Cartright or Omar Sharif or everybody's long-lost favorite grandfather who died trying, or even the much maligned Charles Manson, if he'd only smile and without the swastika, of course. During the lifetime of our childhoods this picture remains, enabling all children who listen with their hearts to hear the words of God. It is sort of like the teddy bear talking to the little girl.

As we grow older the picture of God becomes faded and coffee-stained and fuzzier and maybe we start to carry it in our wallets instead of our hearts. By the time most of us reach middle age we've long ago forgotten what God looks like or why we wanted to know in the first place. Thus you can imagine how mildly disconcerted I was when we finally walked in for our audience with God and I noticed that he was pretty much a dead ringer for Bryant Gumbel.

At precisely the same moment the cat stepped on my scrotum, I heard God shouting: "Throw down that fucking puppet head!" As I sat up on the davenport, I remembered thinking how peculiar it was that, instead of coming from above, the voice appeared to be coming from somewhere below. The voice also sounded rather familiar.

"Throw down that fuckin' puppet head!!" it shouted again.

I got up, gathered the puppet head off the mantel, walked over and opened the kitchen window, and I did.

173

39

" Y O U dig up the passports," said Rambam, "wash off the plastic Baggie, and bring them here to the kitchen counter."

"And what are you going to do?"

"Find the fucking transmitter. If there is one."

"I've never shirked from a Gandhi-like assignment," I said. "But why do *I* have to wash off the Baggie? I never realized you were such a squeamish little baby."

"I'm a squeamish little baby, all right. I'm the kind of squeamish little baby who could twist somebody's head off in about two seconds. Especially if they call me a squeamish little baby."

"All you got to do is take a spatula—if I *had* a spatula—"

"I don't even want to hear about it. Just get the fucking passports out here. And be sure and wash the Baggie with hot water. Modern science has no idea what medieval diseases may be lurking in that cat litter tray. When was the last time you changed it?"

"Oh, it's been several years."

"You've got to be shitting me."

"No one's shitting anyone."

"Somebody's shitting somebody. There's dried cat turds all over the loft. Even the cat thinks that litter tray's disgusting."

"That's not true. The cat knows that after a short period of time cat shit hardens. After a few thousand years it turns into coal and from there, who knows? Like the Billy Joe Shaver song: 'A cat turd's gonna be a diamond some day.'"

"That's not how it goes."

"I'm paraphrasing."

"How about paraphrasing us a little espresso. This could be a long, tedious job."

"It's already a long, tedious conversation," I said, as I opened diplomatic relations with the espresso machine. "And you still don't understand the cat's basic *raison d'Nixon.*"

"Which is?"

"A cry for help. She's angry and upset because I placed a foreign object—the passports—in the cat litter tray."

"So she shits all over the loft to try to signal the sensitive pet owner to take those fucking passports out of the fucking litter box and bring them here into the fucking kitchen before *I* shit all over the loft!"

It was very probably an idle threat, but I made a small show of opening drawers in the kitchen, looking for an appropriate implement. I settled at last upon the boning knife. Then I headed boldly into the rain room. When I returned with the passports in hand, Rambam was sitting at the kitchen table sipping an espresso and the cat had taken another rather theatrically placed dump right in front of the dancing flames of the fireplace.

"Jesus Christ," said Rambam. "How can you live like this?"

"You call this living?" I said.

With the cool demeanor of a surgeon, using only a sharp

pocketknife, Rambam spent the better part of the next hour delicately poking, slicing, and testing the stiff backs of his little passport patients. I sat at the desk, smoking a cigar, sipping espresso, and several times during the entire operation making brief forays to spirit away the occasional dry cat turd on the tip of the ubiquitous boning knife.

"There's a little secret to this," said Rambam, as if lecturing a group of eager young interns. "Make very small incisions and always cut with the grain."

"There's a little secret to this," I said, walking by on my way to the trash can with a cat turd impaled on the tip of the boning knife. "Wait until they're completely dry, then stab 'em in the middle like a shish kebab."

"How long does it usually take them to dry?" asked Rambam conversationally, keeping his attention entirely focused on his work.

"Not as long as it's taking you to find that transmitter," I said.

"If there is one," said Rambam.

"You understand," I said to the cat, "what the crazy man is telling us. If he finds a transmitter the size of a credit card in one of these passports, it means the man who was shot on the dump machine was trying to infiltrate the terrorist cell."

"Or," said Rambam, "he was trying to go shopping at Saks Fifth Avenue."

In a matter of mere moments later, Rambam was seen by myself and the cat performing sort of a modified Jewish-Italian Zorba the Greek dance, holding a small object that looked very much indeed like a credit card high over his head. The cat was somewhat ambivalent about the situation, being highly absorbed simultaneously with both the mysterious object and the choreography. I was highly absorbed with the mildly unnerving notion that men might need to be called to take Rambam away to wig city.

176

"That was a nice version of *Riverdance,*" I said sometime later, as I poured out two strong bolts of Jameson's into two hideously inappropriately stemmed receptacles, my old *Imus in the Morning* coffee mug and a nearby, rather dysfunctional object that, in another, more suburban world, might've been a soap dish. I saluted the puppet head, Rambam toasted the cat, then both of us poured that Irish nectar down our necks.

"All right," said Rambam in a more serious tone. "I'll take the transmitter with me when I leave here tonight. That ought to cut you some slack and send these guys on a wild goose chase."

"Good."

"You realize, of course, that with the transmitter traveling with me, whoever's trying to monitor or infiltrate the cell will probably not be bothering you anymore."

"Good."

"It also means that if anyone now comes by looking for the passports, he's definitely a hard-core Islamic terrorist."

"Not good."

"I'd also suggest you move the passports from the rain room to somewhere else. Whoever shot the guy on the pot is now aware of their approximate location. So put them somewhere else."

"I'll just retain them between my cheeks for the next six months."

"That'll make it difficult to take a dump, but with your current plumbing apparatus so recently having been occupied by the deceased, it seems almost sacrilegious to take a dump under any circumstances. Maybe you can just refrain from dumping for six months."

"Maybe the *cat* can refrain from dumping for six months."

"Getting back to something almost as serious," said Rambam, "we can conclude that the terrorists killed the guy on the toilet, but that doesn't tell us whether the guy was with Mossad, or the

CIA, or the State Department, or maybe some other international agency like Interpol. I know you think little black helicopters are flying around in my brain, but now maybe you'll realize that any of these is a legitimate possibility."

Rambam stopped briefly to pour us both another round. We killed the shots and I fired up a fresh Cuban Montecristo No. 2 and sent a small column of fragrant smoke streaming toward the mercifully silent lesbian dance class. Rambam was staring at me rather intently.

"You realize, of course, that I've already spoken to my contacts. If I just knew to my own satisfaction that the victim was an Israeli, I could relay that information to them. In that case, acting in good faith, they would relieve us of the passports and intercede through whatever channels they felt appropriate. Without evidence that the guy was one of theirs, however, they don't want to step on the toes of the State Department or the CIA. The transmitter shows that the guy was on the side of international law and order. I just can't prove that he was an Israeli."

I sat down at my desk and blew another purple plume of smoke upward to what heavens there were. I put my feet up on the desk comfortably and proceeded to semiconsciously stroke the cat.

"Maybe I can," I said.

40

I put the passports in Sherlock Holmes's head. Then I locked the door, killed the lights, and went to bed. The cat, the passports, and myself, I figured, were about as safe as anything or anyone else in New York at night. I wasn't worried. The important things in life can never be stolen: either they're already gone or you haven't got them yet.

Just before I fell into a fitful sleep I found myself wondering what Sherlock was thinking. With all those passports and Cuban cigars snuggled together inside his head, it was hard to tell. Maybe he was dreaming of being back on Baker Street in his comfortable chair having a smoke. Maybe he was traveling all alone across time and geography. But porcelain heads never tell you what they're thinking. Porcelain eyes never cry. They're almost human in a way.

In the morning, still dressed in my purple Peace Corps sarong and a green Tulane Law sweatshirt, I fed the cat, fed the espresso machine, and located one of Castro's dead soldiers in the trash

179

can, which I quickly resurrected with a kitchen match. Then I wandered over to the desk, lifted Sherlock's little deerstalker, and peered into his cerebral cavity to check on the passports.

"Still there," I shouted to the cat. The cat, of course, said nothing at all. Unlike Ratso, she was not the kind of person who would ever attempt to speak with her mouth full.

"If I keep moving these passports around enough," I said, "maybe I'll forget where they are."

The cat did not respond to that particular ejaculation either, but the phones rang and that gave me something to do. Sadly, watching phones ring is not as much fun as it used to be. In the days before answering machines and voice mail, you could generate a real battle of the wills between the caller and yourself. It was all or nothing. If you watched the phones ring long enough, the person would hang up and you'd probably never find out who you didn't want to speak to. If, in a moment of weakness, you picked up the blower, they had you. Around the ninth ring I had a moment of weakness and I collared the blower on the left. Sure enough, they had me.

"This is the State Department calling," said a voice that could've moonlighted as a recorded announcement at LAX. "To whom am I speaking?"

"Rear Admiral Rumphumper," I said.

I took a sip of espresso and paced myself with a patient puff on the cigar. I blew a cool column of smoke in the general direction of the rain room.

"I'm looking for a Mr. Kinky Friedman," said the joyless voice on the blower.

"He jumped ship last Yom Kippur."

"Make sure he's there at eleven-thirty," said the anonymous asshole at the State Department. Then he terminated the connection.

"It's not often we get visitors at the hospital," I said to the cat.

Alas, the cat did not respond. She didn't like visitors and she didn't like hospitals and she didn't even like me very much at the moment. I couldn't understand why. Just because Stephanie and Khadija had blown me off was no reason for a fucking female feline to try to go for the hat trick.

There wasn't a hell of a lot of time until eleven-thirty and there wasn't a hell of a lot to do with what time there was. What the hell, I thought. Let the State Department come to Mohammed. It was an unfortunate, if somewhat prophetic, choice of proverb, but God only knew what I could do about it now other than roll it into suppository form and fly far above the lesbian dance class to some distant glinting, twenty-four-hour Pakistani moon.

I waited.

At precisely eleven-thirty a mysterious black sedan swam into my vision past a large lethargic pod of garbage trucks. The sedan parked on the sidewalk directly below the fourth-floor window of my kitchen and spit out a matching pair of suits and sunglasses. In a New York nanosecond both pairs of sky-shooters had me in their sights.

I plucked the puppet head from the top of the refrigerator, opened the window, and tossed Yorick out into the cold, brittle Manhattan morning. The two agents watched him fall like they were wishing on a star. In spite of the parachute, the little black puppet head landed with a rather unpleasant bounce or two on the sidewalk and then rolled somewhat pathetically into the gutter before one of the men had the decency to retrieve it.

"A puppet head's a terrible thing to waste," I said to the cat, as I angrily closed the window.

While the cat did not respond, she evidently wholeheartedly agreed with my sentiments for she leapt down from her perch on the windowsill, scampered determinedly across the living room, and began laying some serious Atlantic cable against the far wall of the loft. She was in the very process of this somewhat melo-dramatic catharsis when the two agents came waltzing in the door. One carried a briefcase and the other a slightly bruised puppet head.

"Mr. Friedman," said one of them disgustedly, "did you see what your cat just did?"

"Of course! It's performance art!" I ejaculated cheerfully. "I'm trying to get her a federal grant."

"Maybe we can help you," said the agent.

41

I T didn't take me long to realize that these guys had asshole written all over them. They had all the worst qualities of cops without possessing any of the earthy semicharm of a Fox or a Cooperman. They were educated, officious, polished, and practical—all the bad things. They glibly identified themselves as Agents Wilson and Carter and made it clear that they had come to relieve me of the passports. If they'd only asked me nicely I might've even given them to them. But there was one little point that was bothering me.

"How'd you know about the passports?" I asked.

"The same way we know a lot of things about you, Mr. Friedman," said Agent Wilson smugly.

"And one of the things we know," put in Agent Carter, "is that this time you're going to cooperate."

When there's nothing to say, it's usually a good time not to say it. So I offered the two agents some espresso. They declined. I asked them if they wanted to sit down. They declined. Then I sat down at my desk and relit my cigar and wondered what would happen next. That was when they hit me with the warrant.

"Here's a federal warrant, my friend," said Agent Wilson, as he Frisbeed an official-looking document onto the desk in front of me. "It's a warrant for the seizure of your cat litter box."

"Hold the weddin'," I said, as I started to make a small show of reading the ridiculous document.

"*You* hold the weddin'," said Agent Wilson, taking a step closer to me. "You can also just keep your seat, mister. I'll stay right here to keep you company while Agent Carter takes custody of the evidence covered in this warrant."

"And you're sure you don't want an espresso," I said. Agent Wilson again declined.

Somewhere in this world there was a judge in his black cloak "all deep and distinguished" who'd recently signed a warrant for the seizure of a cat litter tray. Somewhere there was a beautiful woman who was afraid to come in from the cold. Somewhere children were laughing. Somewhere men were gay. Somewhere, unfortunately, was beginning to sound a hell of a lot like New York.

I tried to make a little small talk with Agent Wilson, but apparently all the lines were down. The only circumstances under which I'd ever consider handing over the passports to the State Department would be if doing so would save Khadija from an unfortunate demise, or if it would get my own tail out of a crack about six miles wide. Neither result seemed likely, so I just sat tight, puffed a cigar, studied my empty espresso cup, and listened to my nose hairs grow. For his part, Agent Wilson moved still closer to the desk and began to admire the porcelain head of Sherlock Holmes that resided there.

"That's a handsome bust of Sherlock Holmes," he said. "Where'd you get it?"

"At a garage sale on Jupiter," I said. "Why don't you just take that, too?"

"Because it would constitute an illegal seizure."

"A technicality."

"Not for me, my friend. Not for someone who's sworn to uphold the law."

"Which has got to be better than what Agent Carter's upholding."

As we watched, Agent Carter came stumbling out of the rain room lugging a large, unwieldy object entirely wrapped in several layers of black plastic garbage bags. He did not appear to be greatly enjoying his work. More importantly, he obviously hadn't bothered building enough castles in the cat litter to realize that the passports were no longer there.

"If you have any further questions," said Agent Wilson, as he walked to the door with the heavily encumbered Agent Carter, "you'll find the phone numbers on the warrant for the U.S. Attorney's Office or the Office of—"

"That won't be necessary," I said. "But, I do have one little problem."

"What is it?" asked Agent Wilson.

"Sitting on the edge of my seat for so long is starting to put a permanent wrinkle in my ass."

42

I T ' S not as easy as you might think to find a cat litter tray in
New York City. Cat litter trays like to live in places like Lake
McFuckhead, Texas, or maybe in Burma before it became Myan-
mar where the military government outlawed cat litter trays and
now everybody knows they're full of shit. As for New York, the
city's too big, too refined, too sophisticated, and too busy for anyone to worry about locating cat litter trays. If you're a cat in New
York you'd better learn to shit on the run. If you're a human and
you live in New York and you're in the market for a cat litter tray,
you've got a mighty tall mountain to climb in order to find one,
and, of course, when you finally reach the top you realize that
the mountain itself is made up entirely of cat shit because it's almost impossible in New York to find a cat litter tray.

I decided maybe Ratso could help me find one of those cute
little yuppie stores in SoHo called "Cat Litter Trays & Such." I
hadn't spoken to Ratso since the night Stephanie hosed Count
Your Money at the Carlyle Hotel and I was starting to almost

miss him. Ratso, that is, not the count. So I picked up the blower on the left and reached out to touch the Rat.

"What's wrong with your old cat litter box?" Ratso wanted to know when he came on the line. "It's not time to change the box *or* the litter yet. Seven years isn't up, Kinkstah."

"I'm aware of that, Watson. I tried to tell that to the two agents from the State Department when they came by this morning and took it away. They were under the misguided impression that deep within the layers of litter the missing passports would be gleaming like emeralds under the sea."

"Ah, Sherlock! You've moved the passports!"

"Does nothing get past you, Watson? Of course, I've moved the fucking passports."

"Where to?"

"Never end a sentence with a preposition."

"Okay. Where to, numb-nuts?"

"Look, Ratso, I'll make you a deal. Since you're the most inquisitive person on the planet, I'll tell you—and only you—where I've hidden the passports if you'll help me find a cat litter tray. Is it a deal?"

"It's a deal, Kinkstah! Not only that, but I know where we can get one. There's a guy upstairs, kind of an eccentric schoolteacher named Cecil Hausenfluck. I think you met him. Do you remember?"

"'Am I being rude, Mother?'"

"That's him. Anyway, his cat ran away years ago but he still keeps the litter box."

"He lives in hope? He thinks the cat's coming back?"

"No. He thinks the cat's still there."

"If he thinks the cat's still there, how're you going to get a wing-nut like that to part with the litter box?"

"Trade it for the Virgin Mary. He's always coveted my statue of the Virgin Mary."

"You'd give up that beautiful life-size plaster statue of the Virgin Mary just to help a friend in need of a litter box?"

"Why not?" said Ratso. "I've got eleven more in storage."

It didn't really surprise me. As well as being the most *in*quisitive person on the planet, Ratso was also the most *ac*quisitive. There were some things in life, of course, that even Ratso didn't have. He didn't have, for instance, a guy blown away on his toilet yesterday morning.

"Tell you what, Sherlock. I'll negotiate with Hausenfluck, I'll get the litter tray, and I'll bring it over to your place later this afternoon, but I'm not going to lug that cat litter all over town. So you get the litter, I'll get the tray."

"Sounds like a country song."

By the time I hung up with Ratso, the mood around the loft had lightened considerably. With the plastic cat box virtually in hand, going out and buying a bag of cat litter would be a piece of cake. I threw on my hat and my coat and told the cat she was in charge. Just before I left, I grabbed a few cigars out of Sherlock's head, and while I was grabbing I checked to see if the passports were still there. They were, of course.

"Still *there!*" I shouted in a manner designed largely to irritate the cat.

The cat did not respond. She never responded when she was in charge. I left to get the litter and was already in the hallway when I heard the phones ringing frantically back on my desk. I hurriedly unlocked the door, rushed over to the desk, and hoisted the blower on the left.

"Start talkin'," I said.

"For what it's worth, you were right," said Detective Sergeant Buddy Fox. "Of course, it's probably not worth a hell of a lot."

"The way things are going I'll take what I can get. What was I right about?"

"The prints, pal. We haven't ID'd them yet but they're all over your fuckin' apartment. And they're on that friggin' mazola thing, too."

"Mezuzah."

"Gezundheit! I hope you're happy. Fox the friendly policeman is now five minutes late to eat a corned beef sandwich in a squad car."

I thanked Fox, cradled the blower, and walked over to the counter where I poured a shot of Jameson's into the old bull's horn and then down my neck, almost drowning my uvula in the hasty process. I felt like doing squat-thrusts in the parking lot but I was afraid of getting backed into by a garbage truck. So I called Rambam and told him what I now knew. It wasn't much, but it might be all we needed to put the passports in the right hands.

"You had Fox dust a mezuzah?" said Rambam incredulously.

"He calls it a mazola."

"That's extremely funny."

"I thought you'd like that," I said. "Do you want to hear something else funny?"

"If you insist."

"The dead guy's prints are on the mezuzah."

Rambam was silent for so long that I thought he might've passed away. Being of the Jewish persuasion, we both understood what the evidence meant. If you're not a member of the tribe, of course, you probably wouldn't know that many Jews make a practice of kissing the mezuzah every time they enter a doorway. Technically, what they do is touch their fingers to their lips, then reach up and touch the mezuzah. Since State Department agent-types and CIA operatives are invariably goyim, this pretty conclusively proved that the guy who got whacked on my dumper was an Israeli.

189

"It's good enough for me," said Rambam at last, "and I'll bet it's good enough for the boys in Tel Aviv. I'll call them now and see how they want to handle it. By the way, the idea of dusting the mezuzah is pretty damn funny, but it's also pretty damn clever of you, Kinky."

"That's why they give me the corner office," I said.

43

L U G G I N G a twenty-five-pound bag of cat litter up eight flights of stairs is not as much fun as you might think. Nevertheless, we all have responsibilities in life. Some people have to save their money for college. Some have mortgages to pay. Divorced guys have alimony. Married men simply turn everything over to the War Department. Some men support their families. Some support causes, or parties, or foreign governments. Some support their balls with banana hammocks. I appreciated all their support and I was very grateful to God, Allah, and Ol' Man River that my only responsibility in life was to buy cat litter every seven years and all I had to carry was twenty-five pounds unless you wanted to count the recent rhesus monkey on my back that was masturbating rather wildly at the moment.

The monkey, of course, was the passports. If Rambam didn't get the baton passed to the Israelis pretty damn quick, there was no doubt in my mind that the State Department boys would not be taking any shit from me the next time around. And in the shadow of all this mess lurked the terrorists themselves. I didn't know whether to be worried or relieved that I hadn't heard from Khadija. Maybe the kidnapping of her brother was just another ploy. Maybe the terrorists *had* been using her just to seduce me into giving up the passports. If, indeed, that had been their plan, they had failed. But terrorists, like cats, are persistent little boogers. If a terrorist or a cat wants something, they usually don't stop until they get it. The only reason I hadn't been croaked by the terrorists yet was that they still didn't know where I'd hidden the passports. If they found out, they'd probably whack me. Then the cat would probably eat my body.

"Well, it's good to have something to look forward to," I said, as I entered the loft and looked around for the cat.

The cat was curled, rather cosmically, I thought, around the porcelain bust of Sherlock Holmes. I set down the bag of cat litter, walked over to the desk, lifted Sherlock's little deerstalker cap, and peeped into the smoke and miles and dreams that were his brains. Everything was as it should be. I thought about annoying the cat with another "Still there!" riff but decided to let it slide. She'd been on a tear with the Nixon campaign and I didn't want to further antagonize her.

"Now all we have to do," I told her, "is wait for Ratso to show up with the litter tray and Rambam to talk to his contacts in Tel Aviv and maybe this whole nightmare will be over. Maybe Stephanie will realize she really needs the Kinkster. Maybe you'll stop dumping and I'll start humping."

The cat looked at me with pity in her eyes. Even I knew that I didn't have a lot going on for myself at the moment. Maybe I hadn't hit bottom yet but my personal and my professional lives had somehow managed to hit the same serious speed bump. I was going too fast to be moving this slow. Waiting for Ratso to bring over a cat litter tray was not what I always wanted to do in my life. It was a shining symbol of quiet desperation. It was like measuring your life in decaffeinated coffee spoons.

Around five bells I was in a coma on the davenport when there came a hideous slamming noise that penetrated deeply into my very essence and shattered my dreams before I'd even decided whether or not I wanted them to come true. It was the second power napus interruptus I'd experienced in as many days and it proved to be extremely unsettling to my rather precarious emotional state. I sat up like a zombie on a crooked couch, bloodshot roulette eyes vainly striving to penetrate the gathering gloom. At last I saw him.

Standing on the fire escape, barely four feet away from my head, was a man in a raccoon skin coat, purple boots, and what looked like a William Holden drinking helmet, repeatedly slamming a large pink oblong object against the rusty, reverberating bars of the fire escape. It took me longer than it should have to identify the man as Ratso and the object as the much awaited cat litter tray.

"Open the fuckin' window before the terrorists come and get me!" shouted Ratso.

"No self-respecting terrorist would come near a man in that outfit," I said, as I opened the window. "Especially one armed with a cat litter tray. Even terrorists fear the insane."

"I must be insane to come over here. I heard that a guy got blown away on your pot the other morning. Did that really happen? Where are you hiding the passports, Kinkstah?"

"How'd you know about the guy on the pot?"

"I have my sources."

Ratso pronounced the word "sources" the same way normal Americans would say "sauces." Of course, normal Americans don't usually dress like Ratso, nor would they usually enter your apartment from the fire escape. Nor would they fling the litter tray on your desk, walk right over and open the refrigerator, find nothing to their liking and open the freezer compartment, and take out an innocent-looking jar of mayonnaise.

"What the hell *is* this fucking thing?" shouted Ratso.

"I think the terrorists were trying to intimidate me into giving them the passports—"

"It can't be what I think it is!"

"Of course it can. When was the last time you saw a smelt wearing a black onyx ring?"

"It *is* a fucking finger!"

"Ah, Watson, your powers of observation seem only to have sharpened over the years. Age may have affected your beauty, but not your mind."

Ratso was looking even more pale and pallid than usual. I took the jar from his hand, placed it back in the freezer, and closed the freezer door.

"Whoever sent this macabre object wanted me to believe it belonged to Khadija, but I can testify that all her fingers are intact. Unfortunately, now *all* of her has disappeared."

"That fucking finger still belongs to *some*body!" shouted Ratso.

"*Belonged,*" I corrected. "My, aren't we a squeamish little baby."

"If I was a squeamish fucking little baby I'd have mentioned that your living room floor is now mined with cat turds."

"Keeps the terrorists on their toes."

At Ratso's persistent urgings, I revealed to him the current residence of the cache of purloined passports. I even allowed him to remove the stash from Sherlock's head and examine them like a dutiful little Watson. One thing that every private investigator soon learns is that clues, answers, and insights often derive from the most unlikely sources. Or should I say "sauces."

"Look at their eyes," Ratso was saying. "They all look similar.

Maybe a strong family resemblance or it might be something else. They remind me of somebody I know."

"You met Khadija briefly," I said, "right here in the loft that afternoon with Rambam. That's her. There's her brother, Ahkmed. They do bear a strong resemblance."

"The eyes are the same," said Ratso. "Almost all of these passport photos have the same eyes. They've got that dangerous sparkle combined with that sort of sad resignation you often see in martyrs in the making."

"Well spoken, Watson. To me they look like the eyes of people in photographs after they're dead."

"That's it! I know who they remind me of. They remind me of Tom Baker!"

I held several of the passports up to the desk lamp. They were mostly Arab types of course. Baker was about as Irish-American as you could get, possibly too much for his own good. And yet I did see that certain spiritual similarity of which Ratso had spoken.

"Yes, the eyes certainly have it," I said. "The earth-bound beauty. The death-bound glory. Passionate eyes that once might've been loving and now no longer care what pictures life may show them. Yet they are not Tom Baker's eyes, Ratso. Even in death, even in careless, reckless life, even when he didn't give a damn, Tom Baker's eyes were smiling."

"But you're not going to be smiling, Sherlock, when these bastards come to reclaim their passports. Maybe you should come stay with me again. As you may have noticed, I'm leaving immediately."

"These goddamn passports have been lying around here forever. Tonight, with any luck, I'll be fobbing them off on Rambam, who'll turn them over to his friendly neighborhood Mossad agent. If the bastards have waited this long, what makes you think they're going to strike tonight?"

"Their eyes," said Ratso.

After Ratso bugged out for the dugout, I put Cecil Hausen-fluck's cat litter tray in the bathtub and filled it up with clean, pristine cat litter. The cat watched the operation from the toilet lid where quite recently a man had been bugled to Jesus, or, in light of the latest evidence, to Moses. The cat did not care too much for either Jesus or Moses, if the truth be known. She did, however, in unguarded moments, reveal a lingering, albeit some-what grudging, fondness for St. Francis.

"And now, under cover of darkness," I said to the toilet-bound cat, "I shall proceed with the last, yet far from the least impor-tant phase of this clandestine procedure."

The cat watched as I ankled it out of the rain room only to re-turn moments later bearing a small, plastic-wrapped bundle of passports. As night fell on the city, I buried the bundle deep un-der a sand dune of cat litter. Then I pulled the curtain partway across the shower rod and glanced in the bathroom mirror. If there'd been a Gypsy in that bathroom mirror I'd certainly have wanted to ask his advice. But there was no Gypsy. All I could see on that silver plane was the rather gaunt and haunted face of a middle-aged man and a mildly bored cat sitting behind him on a toilet.

"Lightning and State Department nerds never strike in the same place twice," I said to the cat.

The cat continued to look mildly bored. She seemed to ex-press no interest whatsoever in the fruits of my labors. I hoped the State Department would be equally disinterested. I left the rain room thinking of calling Rambam again, but on second thought headed instead for the bottle of Jameson's. I was pouring a shot into the old bull's horn when I heard a slight noise in the darkened doorway behind me. It was the sound of a door closing quietly. It was my door.

"Salaam," said the thin figure standing stock-still just inside the loft. "My name is Ahkmed."

"I thought you'd been kidnapped," I said, cursing myself for not locking the door after Ratso had left.

Ahkmed looked around the loft with a nonchalance that was almost spooky. Then he took a few steps forward and smiled a crooked smile.

"I escaped," he said.

44

" I don't know what my sister told you," said Ahkmed, "but it is well that you believe what I tell you, my friend. If you do not give us the passports, you will surely die."

Ahkmed was not physically a big man. In fact, he was rather short, rather thin, even almost frail-looking—if you didn't know better. If you didn't know that round and round in his veins ran a cold, desperate cornered rat of hatred that already had eaten away his heart and brain and conscience. I knew he was a coward because all terrorists are cowards. He would kill for no reason except that he couldn't stop the rat.

"Where's Khadija?" I said.

In life I've always believed you should be weak enough to be afraid, but strong enough to let it show. With a potentially violent confrontation such as this, however, bluff is everything. The more conversation, the more eye contact, the more appearance of business as usual that goes down, the better your chances. Otherwise, *you* go down.

"Closer than you think," said Ahkmed. "You will not get away from us."

I poured the contents of the bull's horn down my neck with as much casual cockiness as I could muster. As I placed the empty bull's horn on the counter, I saw Ahkmed pull out a long, shiny knife. Pretending not to notice, but with a slightly shaky hand, I poured two more shots of Jameson's.

"Would you like a drink?" I said.

"I would like not to have to kill you," said Ahkmed.

There is an irrationality that often overrides your being in times of extreme danger. The sensible thing to do would be to give the guy his precious fucking passports and hope that he'd go with Allah and get the hell out of my loft and my life. But some Jewish-American Jiminy Cricket inside my soul would not let me do that.

"Your last chance," said Ahkmed, moving up to the counter, holding the knife gently in his hand like a small bird. "The passports. We know they're here. Where are they?"

"I gave them to the State Department."

"That's the last lie you will ever tell," he said.

Like a deadly dance step, he made a fluid lunge which I countered by stepping away, although not quite quickly enough. The knife slashed my left wrist as Ahkmed's free hand found my neck and both of us fell with a crash across the kitchen table. I took a deep breath, tucked my chin to fend off the strong, thin fingers around my throat, and with both hands grabbed for the wrist of the knife-wielding hand of the assassin. He was, as I soon found out, surprisingly strong for his size.

He let go of my windpipe and before I knew it, both of his hands were occupied with the task of powering the knife into my throat. Through some instinctive love of life, I twisted my body upon the tabletop causing the legs to collapse, which sent both of us crashing violently to the floor. Someone in the heavens above Winnie Katz sent the knife skittering under the couch, leaving the two of us struggling back and forth across the floor, rolling obliviously through a sea of blood and dust and cat turds. If he'd still had the knife, I thought, I'd probably be many stories above Winnie Katz right now. But he didn't have the knife, and if I didn't bleed to death, I would survive this experience like Tom Baker weathering a barroom brawl. How strange, I reflected, as he tried to slam my head against the floor, that only two nights ago I was rolling in his sister's arms.

Suddenly a little white ball of fluff came tearing by to my right. Like a character in a dream, I recognized Baby Savannah Samet, Stephanie's beautiful white Maltese. Only it wasn't a dream. Baby Savannah put on the brakes, skidded a few yards, then began running rapid circles around Ahkmed and myself. In a moment, Stephanie's two other *enfants*, Pyramus and Thisbe, were running madly about the loft, ice-picking my brain with their high-pitched yipping and yapping. To this was added a rather horrifying howling sound that emanated, quite obviously, from the unseen cat.

"Dickhead!" shouted Stephanie's shrill voice from the other side of the counter. "This place has always looked like crap, but I've never seen it with cat shit all over the floor! It's pathetic! Dickhead! Where are you, Dickhead!"

Even with our cultural and ideological differences, it was mildly embarrassing for me, in front of Ahkmed, to have to answer to the name "Dickhead." It was one of those little things, however, that you just learned to put up with if you wanted Stephanie DuPont in your life. At this moment in particular, I very much wanted her in my life, so I gave what I suppose was a muffled shout and, like two boys caught fighting at recess by the teacher, the terrorist and I disentangled ourselves just as Stephanie rounded the kitchen counter and spotted us.

"What are you two fucks doing down there?" she shouted. "Jerkin' each other off?"

I don't know how Ahkmed felt, but being insulted by a gorgeous, glorious nine-foot-three blonde in red stilettos made me somewhat ambivalent about being an American. If I thought Ahkmed would react violently, I was wrong. He got up with as much dignity as the situation allowed, and began moving quietly for the door.

"Stephanie," I said, still on the floor, motioning toward my fleeing attacker, "I'm not sure that you understand—"

"Shut up, Dickhead!" she said. "Who was that wimpy friend of yours anyway and why were you two rolling around on this filthy floor like a couple of house apes? That sick fucking cat of yours really has to go. Baby Savannah! Get away from the cat turds, darling."

I got up from the floor, made sure Ahkmed had closed the door behind him, locked it, and located a red "Team Bukowski" T-shirt to stem the flow of blood from my wrist. The animals seemed to be settling down a bit and hopefully my pulse would soon be following suit as well. Right now, watching Stephanie bend over to scoop up Baby Savannah, my come count and my adrenaline were both red-lining.

"What happened to your wrist, Dickhead? A failed suicide attempt?"

"Just a little accident," I said. "I was jerking off and my ball blew up."

"I *knew* you two were jerking off! Who *is* that faggy little foreigner anyway?"

"He's a fucking Islamic fundamentalist fucking terrorist named Ahkmed who's probably killed hundreds of people and if he'd found the phony passports I've been hiding he'd no doubt be on his way to killing thousands more."

"You really are *losing* it, *Dick*head! That's r*idic!* In fact, it's beyond r*idic!* It's truly pa*thet!* The whole fucking thing's *sus-pish!* And it's so fucking *sad* that you have to lie."

"Goddamnit!" I said, "when I find that bloody knife under the couch maybe you'll believe me!"

I got down on the floor and, with the help of Pyramus and Thisbe, began checking for the weapon under the couch. It wasn't there.

"Baby," said Stephanie to the little white ball of fluff in her arms, "sick Uncle Kinky's looking for a bloody knife that isn't there. Pyramus and Thisbe are looking, too. But guess what, Baby? No knife. And the terrorist just left with his tail between his legs. Just like in the movies. It's *sad,* really."

"What's sad is that you don't realize that both of our lives were just in danger. This guy had a long knife and very likely an even longer history of international terrorism. These are desperate people and they won't hesitate to kill to achieve their ends. Now that Ahkmed's seen you, you may become a target, too. So I'm warning you. Watch your back."

"I'll let *you* do that," said Stephanie coyly. "It's about the only thing I know you're good at."

"Never end a sentence with a preposition."

"All right. It's about the only thing I know you're good at, Dickhead."

To the relief of the cat and the frustration of myself, Stephanie began gathering up Pyramus and Thisbe and heading for the hallway. Maybe she was just busting my chops, I thought. Maybe she really did believe my rather outlandish-sounding scenario and was just trying to lighten the mood. It would be good to know that I was believed by somebody other than a man with black helicopters flying around in his brain and a man who kept eleven life-sized statues of the Virgin Mary in storage.

"Stephanie," I said. "You *do* believe me?"

"Clap your hands, Baby," she said, "if you believe that international terrorism came to Uncle Kinky's apartment."

Baby Savannah did not clap her hands. The only person in the world I'd gladly die for was now walking out of the loft in her uncaring, disbelieving red stilettos. I found myself doing about the only thing she'd claimed I was good at. Watching her back.

"Hold the weddin'!" I shouted. "You want some evidence that for the past few weeks I've been visited by threats, intimidation, and terrorism? I'll show you something. Just walk over to that refrigerator."

Stephanie was not good at taking directions from men, and particularly from me. But very possibly she now responded to what was a commanding, urgent, deeply masculine tone in my voice. Anyway, she walked over to the refrigerator.

"Open the freezer compartment," I said.

She obeyed.

"Take out the little mayonnaise jar."

She obeyed.

She studied the jar for a few moments, holding it up to the light and peering curiously at its contents. Then she put it back inside the freezer like a shopper in a supermarket placing a piece of unwanted merchandise back on the shelf.

"What is it?" she said. "Your dick?"

45

SOMETIME after Stephanie had flown the coop, I called Rambam to fill him in on the Ahkmed adventure as well as to try to goose him into making the Israeli connection as quickly as possible. He was vastly amused by Stephanie's comments about the filthy condition of the loft as I was struggling for my life in the murderous grip of a terrorist.

"Have you contacted Tel Aviv yet?" I asked.

"Of course. But they're seven hours later than us so I didn't go into detail. It's not like I'm on a first name basis with anyone there. I just left a message and said it was urgent. I should hear from them in the morning. They'll check it out and let me know what steps to take."

"Somebody better take some steps soon," I said. "This whole situation's starting to get up my sleeve."

"Just sit tight, pal. You almost resisted the temptations of a modern-day Mata Hari, you escaped the Raid on Entebbe by grabbing the side of a garbage truck, and now your imperious, high-maintenance girlfriend and her three rodent-size dogs have driven off a bloodthirsty terrorist bent on the destruction of western civilization. Her success in this operation, as I understand it, was thanks to her vitriolic complaints regarding the cat turds that are rather noticeably piling up in your living room."

"That's essentially correct," I said. "But what am I supposed to do now?"

"Try cleaning up the cat turds," said Rambam.

Before he rang off, Rambam promised to call me as soon as he heard from the Israelis. I promised not to masturbate like a monkey while hanging from the shower rod until the situation with the passports was satisfactorily resolved. But I had to admit the loft was pretty quiet after I'd cradled the blower, and not just a little bit spooky. It's very important in circumcisions such as this not to let your imagination veer across the median of reason like a runaway garbage truck. Sometimes a little shot in the dark can help stabilize your emotional ship of state.

"This is a bottle of Gammel Dansk," I said to the cat. "It's a Danish drink sent to me by a Swedish friend named Linus Sjobrandt who works for Scandinavian Air Service. Linus is sometimes known as the Upgrader and right now my spirits could use a little upgrading so I thought I'd try this one. The bottle is quite unusual and so is the drink."

The cat drank all this in with a look of feigned interest bordering on ennui. I did not let her deter my captivating travelogue.

"If you're ever in the Scandinavian countries you should make a point of ordering a few shots of Gammel Dansk. It's a very special kind of drink, the sort of thing that only Europeans would bother to manufacture or appreciate. Americans are almost totally ignorant of the medicinal or spiritual values of Gammel Dansk. All we're good at is watching Stephanie DuPont's back."

A wry, almost sour expression crossed the countenance of the cat. She did not like Stephanie DuPont or Pyramus or Thisbe or Baby Savannah Samet. Nor did she appreciate the medicinal or the spiritual values of Gammel Dansk.

After a few rounds of the drink, which has a bitter, bracing, mildly hallucinogenic quality to it, I found myself energetically shish-kebabbing cat turds off the living room floor with the boning knife. I was deeply involved in this Gandhi-like, decidedly domestic activity when the two red telephones on my desk began ringing like there was no tomorrow. The way things had been going, that was fine with me.

I skipped blithely over to the desk and hefted the blower on the left. The voice, though I hadn't heard it in a while, seemed oddly familiar. I suppose I thought I'd never hear it again.

"Khadija," I said. "Are you all right?"

"I'm better than all right," she said. "Except for the fact that I'm missing you so much. You could crook your finger and destroy my life."

"I've missed you, too," I said. "Where did you go the other morning? Where have you been?"

"I'll tell you all that tonight. But I've been worried about you. I couldn't risk calling until now. Are you okay?"

"I'm fine. I met your brother."

"You met—Ahkmed? He's *alive?* He's all *right?*"

"He sends his love."

Khadija was calling from the Gramercy Park Hotel. From room 504. From a beautiful old canopy bed, she said. She was very relieved that her brother was safe and sound. She needed me now. She wanted me in her arms, between her legs. She wanted me to take her completely tonight. She loved me, she said. Totally.

With a boning knife full of cat turds in one hand, a bull's horn full of Gammel Dansk in the other, a cigar in my mouth, and still sporting a monstro-erection from my phone call with Khadija, I was a man who'd already made the decision I had to make. If I had to rent a pair of Rollerblades. If I had to crawl across eight miles of flat rock. Even if I had to take the subway. I was going to the Gramercy Park Hotel.

You never know what you're going to find when you go out at night in New York. You don't know if you'll find love, danger, happiness, or hell. You don't even know if you'll find a cab. But you're ready to take your chances. That's why you live in New York.

It was pushing eleven-thirty when the hack spit me out in front of the Gramercy. I was familiar with the hotel. I'd hung out there with Abbie Hoffman and with Bob Dylan and the boys. I stayed there with the former Miss Texas the night I kissed her drunken foot in the front seat of Rambam's car as he drove ninety-two miles an hour. I'd died in those rooms, committed suicide several times, written songs, masturbated like a monkey, taken drugs, and dreamed. But tonight could well be a spiritual first for the Kinkster. Tonight I could very well be hosing a terrorist at the Gramercy Park.

But by the time I got into the old elevator at the hotel, I was having my doubts, and by the time it reached the fifth floor, I was riddled with them. When I knocked on room 504, I found that it was occupied by a woman who looked very much like a prostitute and a young guy who looked like a Waycross, Georgia, farm boy. They said Khadija'd left there years ago, looking for some Texas Jewboy. Maybe they didn't actually say anything. Maybe it was just the Gammel Dansk talking. Anyway, I was right about one thing. I'd been hosed.

I hailed a hack back to Hudson, legged it up Vandam, and arrived at the loft around half-past Cinderella time. It was easy to walk in because the door was open. I was not surprised.

Sherlock's gray porcelain eyes seemed to be gazing at me with an inherent, somewhat stern reprimand. The puppet head maintained his stoic smile from the top of the mantelpiece. If the puppet head had had shoulders he probably would've shrugged. The cat was nowhere in sight.

I walked into the rain room with a gnawing sense of foreboding. The cat was there, all right. She seemed to be quite industriously scratching around in what was now a half-empty litter tray. The rest of the fresh litter had been scattered like a sandstorm in the desert across the miles and miles of bathroom tiles on the floor of the rain room. The cat, in her most kvetching mope, could never have made this mess. I checked the litter box just to be sure, but it was exactly as I had suspected. It was exactly what I didn't want to happen.

"It's all yours now," I said to the cat. "The passports are gone."

46

S P R I N G came to New York earlier than usual that year and it was about time. I never heard from Khadija again. Or Ahkmed. Or the State Department. Or the Israelis. I had a pretty good idea who might've taken the passports but with all the parties involved, I couldn't really be absolutely sure. Of course, there are very few things in life about which any of us can be absolutely sure, so I didn't let it bother me too much. Needless to say, I couldn't go to the cops. At least the cat was now back to regularly frequenting the litter box, which was a blessing to me and no doubt a relief to the few intrepid visitors who on rare occasions still dared to drop by the loft.

It must've been several months later when any real closure on the subject of the stolen passports was achieved. Rambam, Ratso, McGovern, and myself were having dinner at Asti's on 12th Street near Fifth Avenue. My special guest of honor that night was one Stephanie DuPont. That was another subject that desperately needed some closure, but I couldn't very well ask her what she did with the count at the Carlyle without revealing that we'd been spying upon her. If she ever found out, a little voice inside me warned that she might become highly agitato.

"Did anything come out of that mess with the terrorists, the State Department, the cops, and the Israelis?" asked McGovern, ever the inquisitive journalist.

"Nothing," I said. "They don't write. They don't call."

"You want to hear my theory about who took the passports?" said Ratso, as he dug heartily into the antipasto.

"No," said Rambam.

"How do we know there were any passports?" said Stephanie. "How do we know there were ever any terrorists? Maybe Friedman made it all up as an attention-getting device."

"How intuitive of you to suggest that, darling," I said. "You know I'd be nothing without you."

"You *are* nothing," said Stephanie. "Where's the wine list?"

"It's wonderful to see Stephanie's confidence in you, Kinkstah!" said Ratso. "Have you ever considered that the two of you might possibly comprise what we like to call a 'sick relationship'?"

"You're probing in the general area of the wound," I said. "Maybe our relationship needs counseling."

"Our relationship doesn't need counseling," said Stephanie. "Our relationship needs a taxidermist. Where the hell's the wine list?"

"Ratso ate it," I said.

"Waiter," said Stephanie. "Give us two bottles of your finest champagne."

"Who's paying?" asked Rambam.

"I am," I said. "I want people to like me."

"Well, it isn't working," said Stephanie.

"What're we celebrating?" asked McGovern.

"Who cares?" said Rambam.

"We're celebrating Stephanie getting rid of that phony fucking count," said Ratso.

"Which is better than Stephanie going down for the count," I said.

"You're hangin' by spit, Friedman," said Stephanie.

"Here's to eighty-sixing the phony count," said McGovern, as he lifted his champagne glass, "and the Renoir which was probably phony, too!"

"How'd you know about the Renoir?" Stephanie asked McGovern.

"A good reporter never divulges his sauces," said Ratso, rushing to cover McGovern's little miscue.

"In McGovern's case," I said, "they really *are* sauces."

"A good reporter keeps his fucking mouth shut," said Rambam.

"Anyway," said Ratso, valiantly attempting to move the subject away from the Renoir, "does anyone want to hear my theory about who stole the passports the Kinkstah stole from the terrorists?"

"No," said Rambam. "But as the only licensed private investigator at the table—"

"With a satellite dish on your head—" added Stephanie sweetly.

"—I'll tell you what I believe really happened," said Rambam, glowering at Stephanie.

"We all know what happened," said Ratso, as he poured another round of champagne for himself and, as an afterthought, for the rest of the table. "That fucking Arab chick—what was her name?—Khadija—suckered Sherlock here out of the loft, and while he was gone she stole the passports."

"There *was* no Arab chick," said Rambam.

"Of course there was," said Ratso. "I saw her. You saw her, too, didn't you, Kinkstah? In fact, you did more than see her."

"That figures," said Stephanie.

"There was *no* Arab chick," said Rambam demonstratively. "I've given it a lot of thought in the past few months and this is the only way it could've worked. Kinky meets Khadija on the plane. She goes to the lavatory as the plane is descending into La Guardia. Somehow she walks right by Kinky without him seeing her, leaves her bag, and he, being a stupid southern gentleman, takes it home with him. That's one question I asked. How'd she get by him on the plane?"

Nobody had any answers to that, so McGovern poured everybody another round as Rambam held the floor and I held my breath. Rambam continued.

"Without getting needlessly graphic with a lady present—"

"There's a lady present?" I said.

"—Who's about to put your dick in the Cuisinart," said Stephanie.

"Without getting needlessly graphic with a *lady* present," Rambam persevered, "Kinky had a perfect opportunity to hose Khadija and only wound up with a blow job."

"That figures," said Stephanie.

"Yes, it does," said Rambam, "but very possibly not in the way you think. Aside from the passports, we found some pretty kinky things, as it were, in that little pink suitcase. Now Kinky spent another night with Khadija and reported to me that he received a hand job—"

"—Is this really necessary?" asked Stephanie.

"Absolutely," said Rambam.

"Abso*lute*ly," said McGovern, apparently enjoying the champagne as much as the discussion.

"Now the two times Khadija was in Kinky's loft were just prior to the period when Kinky's cat assertively went on what Kinky himself describes as 'a vindictive dumping campaign'—"

"Would you care to order, miss?" said the waiter, suddenly appearing over Stephanie's trim shoulder. She shuddered briefly.

"Give us a little more time," she said.

"So Khadija saw no cat turds around the loft," Rambam rolled on relentlessly. "This is very important to remember because by the time Ahkmed came by, some days later, there was cat shit everywhere you looked."

"Of course there was," I said, defending the cat in her absence. "I'd moved the passports back to the litter box from Sherlock Holmes's head. The cat, quite naturally and instinctively resented having foreign objects secreted in the cat litter. She went on a major cable-laying crusade."

"But Khadija was gone by then," said Rambam. "She didn't know that. So she couldn't have made the connection that the passports were hidden in the cat litter. And the State Department didn't take them because they weren't going to be burned by the old empty cat litter box trick twice. And the Israelis didn't take the passports because they were already missing before they even called me back. So that just leaves Khadija and Ahkmed and neither of them had complete enough data on the evolving cat turd situation to put it all together."

"So maybe Ahkmed called Khadija," I said, "and they compared notes."

"Impossible," said Rambam.

"Why impossible?" I asked.

"Don't you see it *yet*, Dickhead?" said Stephanie.

"See what?"

"Of course, I can't prove it," said Rambam.

"Prove what?"

"It doesn't really matter," said Rambam. "You were under a

213

lot of stress being saddled with those passports for so long and now none of us will probably ever know their true purpose. But it's the only real scenario that fits. And the Israelis, at least, were able to confirm my suspicions about Ahkmed."

"Which were?"

"That he's an extremely intelligent, dangerous, duplicitous master of disguise."

"And Khadija?" I asked in a hoarse whisper.

"There *is* no Khadija," said Rambam. "They're really the same person, and that person is Ahkmed."

"Impossible," I said, but I knew it wasn't.

Stephanie stood up from the table, her movements a bit wobbly. I wasn't sure if she was extremely angry or extremely disgusted, but whichever it was, it was glorious to behold. The opera singers on the little stage nearby couldn't hold a candle to her. Unfortunately, they had just completed their aria when Stephanie intoned in a hauntingly shrill voice her parting words.

"Ahkmed's a transvestite, you're a fag, and I'm leaving!"

She tossed her blond, rich girl hair over her shoulder, and on red stiletto heels and legs as long as forever, she marched out of the restaurant without a backward glance.

"Beautiful as dogs playing poker," said McGovern admiringly.

"I don't think she's going to be kissing your mezuzah anytime soon," said Rambam.

"She'll be back," I said. "She forgot her purse and I've taken something out of it she'll be needing."

"What is it?" asked Ratso.

"Her passport," I said.

47

" I F there's one thing I hate," I said to the beautiful woman on the airplane, "it's meeting a beautiful woman on an airplane."

"How terrible for you," she said, briefly looking up from her FAA-mandated copy of Danielle Steel's latest novel. The sleeves of her blouse were thin green stems. Her hands, holding the book, were fragile, off-white flowers bathed in the moonlight of memory. It was morning. It was summertime. I was flying back to Texas.

"Will you keep an eye on this bag?" said the woman. "I'll be right back."

After she'd gone, a flight attendant came by with a batch of newspapers and I took one at random and unfolded it. As long as I live I'll never forget the headline. It read: TWA FLIGHT 800 BLOWN FROM THE SKIES. TERRORISM SUSPECTED.